About the Author

The author is an English teacher with a keen interest in mysteries in all their manifestations. He has lived and worked both in the UK as well as abroad, especially Istanbul, Turkey. He is married with a son.

True Ghost Stories Vol. 1

Jonathan Stanyer

True Ghost Stories Vol. 1

Olympia Publishers
London

www.olympiapublishers.com
OLYMPIA PAPERBACK EDITION

Copyright © Jonathan Stanyer 2021

The right of Jonathan Stanyer to be identified as author of
this work has been asserted in accordance with sections 77 and 78
of the Copyright, Designs and Patents Act 1988.

All Rights Reserved

No reproduction, copy or transmission of this publication
may be made without written permission.
No paragraph of this publication may be reproduced,
copied or transmitted save with the written permission of the
publisher, or in accordance with the provisions
of the Copyright Act 1956 (as amended).

Any person who commits any unauthorised act in relation to
this publication may be liable to criminal
prosecution and civil claims for damage.

A CIP catalogue record for this title is
available from the British Library.

ISBN: 978-1-78830-995-0

This is a work of fiction.
Names, characters, places and incidents originate from the writer's
imagination. Any resemblance to actual persons, living or dead, is
purely coincidental.

First Published in 2021

**Olympia Publishers
Tallis House
2 Tallis Street
London
EC4Y 0AB**

Printed in Great Britain

Acknowledgements

Acknowledgements to the front cover photograph (Roxana Tohaneanu-Shields) with a caption 'According to the Spiritual Centre website, a robin encountered in a graveyard symbolises the continuing presence of a deceased loved one among the living.'

I want to thank four people for reading and encouraging me in writing.
Philip Gee
Stevie Culhane
James Fountain
Guy Power

1
Soul adrift

'You're going to sleep in here,' Grandma told me, fussing with the small suitcase my mother had given me for my weekend stay. The bedroom was a large first floor room with a bay window overlooking the front garden, hidden from view by a somewhat tatty net curtain.

Walking in, my skin was immediately brushed by something vague, the faintest breath of air. Where had it come from? I thought, immediately standing still. I watched Grandma, who hadn't seemingly noticed anything, as she hurried round the double bed, opened the curtains, and then the old-fashioned window. From my spot I looked around carefully — whatever had touched me had now gone, ironic considering Grandma had opened a window.

From when I was a small boy I could always tell if a room was 'active' for want of a better word — it was not a burden or gift easily discussed — my parents would brush off any mention of my unwanted ability, so it was shrugged off, increasing my overall shyness. Entering a new room in any house, my spine would occasionally bristle warning me that this was a 'busy' room — Grandma's front room was definitely 'busy.'

Night came and I, the somewhat reluctant eight-year-old, went to bed after bidding my grandparents goodnight. I had a radio with me for company which no one was taking off me! Seeing nothing untoward in the now shadowy room lit by a bedside lamp, I climbed into bed and pulled the blankets up. I was soon asleep.

I awoke in the night with the room in darkness. Grandma must have come in and switched off my bedside light. My spine tingled as I switched on the bedside lamp. Sitting up in bed and squinting into the shadows I couldn't see anything — the sideboard with the large mirror stood opposite my bed.

The armchair was drawn up by the window.

The dark wooden wardrobe was on my right against the interior wall.

Heavy fabrics and furnishings covered dark wooden surfaces. Shadowy pictures and photos adorned the walls.

All still.

Apparently.

The tingling had taken over my arms and legs but I still didn't feel scared — more inquisitive in the way of an eight-year-old. I got out of bed and turned on the main room light, but the sensation I was feeling didn't abate. In the chill air, I looked under the bed, and tiptoed round looking in corners, under the armchair, out of the window — looking for a source of this 'signal' — where *was* it coming from?

After some silent inquiry, I came to understand that it, whatever 'it' was, emanated from next to the wardrobe. In particular, my gaze was drawn from the ground and towards the ceiling almost in the top right corner. The energy was stronger here. Feelings of sadness suddenly surrounded me. I started to sigh — my lips quivered. Why?

I didn't like this feeling. I didn't like to feel sad and not know why.

I decided that I had had enough. Turning off the main light, I opened the bedroom door and peered onto the shadowy landing. Pinched by the cold night air, I padded into the third bedroom next to mine — no more than a box room — wherein was a large comfortable armchair. Nestling within it, I was soon asleep with a blanket over me brought from my bed.

I was woken sometime later by my grandma and ushered sleepily back into my bed, just as dawn was breaking. I soon drifted off to sleep again as if what had passed in the night was no more than a dream. There were no admonishments at breakfast. No comment on my night move. It was never spoken about.

Ever.

This became the pattern of my visits to my grandparents unless I was accompanied by one of my siblings. Then thoughts of whatever lurked in the corner of the bedroom subsided under board games and children chat as we slept on either side of the double bed. Later on, as a teenager, my lone visits followed the pattern of disturbed sleep, an awful upsetting energy reaching out from the same corner of the ceiling, and an eventual room move to sleep properly.

My grandparents grew older.

Years passed, and I turned twenty. My granddad was on his deathbed in the same bed I had fitfully slept in for all those years. Myself, my father and uncles had kept a vigil on the last night — me occasionally gazing around a room I had got to know so well, looking for — or rather trying to sense — anything out of the ordinary.

Nothing. In fact, a serene peace had descended on the room as my beloved grandfather passed away.

Later on, after the funeral, I was summoned by my grandma to stay with her a few days to help her sort out granddad's things and do some heavy lifting of books and boxes. I was not looking forward to going, and even more perturbed by my grandma saying I was to sleep in the same bed where my granddad had died. I complained to my parents but, being the eldest grandchild, it was my duty to help out. So, with a heavy heart, I took the two-hour bus trip to her house. After a chatty evening reminiscing and looking through old photos bedtime came, and I prepared for the inevitable pantomime that would follow in the night hours.

I got into bed with my large stereo perched on the chair next to me, ready to drown out any anxieties. Grandma, being quite deaf, wouldn't be bothered by it. I settled down in bed.

An odd thing happened.

Nothing happened.

Nothing active in the room at all — peace all around me.

The next night it continued in the same vein, and the next.

Whatever had been there was there no longer.

I was stumped — but relieved nonetheless.

A few years later, Grandma sold the house and downsized into a bungalow in the city centre. Memories of the room — though not forgotten — were consigned to the past.

One day, several years after she had died, I was working abroad when I received a newspaper cutting from my parents. I read it, immediately overcome by shock as my mouth dropped open. Almost collapsing I sat down before my rubbery legs gave way.

The elderly couple next to my late grandparents' house had also both died, and their house had been sold. The new owners had been clearing out the long-neglected attic. In one dusty, cobwebby corner, they had found an antique wooden box. Opening the box, they found a decayed, faded linen bundle. Among those bandages there were mummified remains of a newborn baby.

I started to cry.

Big tears fell from my eyes as I sobbed in my armchair.

The mystery was solved.

The elderly couple next door, who had seemed perfectly respectable to me and presumably my grandparents, had harboured this dark secret for who knows how long? The cutting said the remains were dated to approximately forty years previously. A period when the elderly couple, who I had frequently seen over my grandparents' garden fence, had been living there. In God's name what had they done and why?

I knew now what a sad, sorrowful entity had been reaching out to me across time, across death. I cried because I hadn't helped. What could a kid like me have done?

Then, the tears of regret I had shed turned to tears of

joy as I realised in my mind how the story had ended. My beloved grandfather had departed his life in that room and taken the little bundle of pain with him to the loving arms of God, freeing it from the earthly torment it had suffered for decades just feet from where my bed had been.

Postscript. Near the end of her life, my grandma had opened up a little about her encounters with the psychic world. She had seen at least one ghost in her bungalow she told me. I told her about some of my experiences, but did not mention my childhood encounters with the unknown in her house.

Then I realised.

For years I had wondered why my grandparents had slept in the back bedroom of their house — clearly smaller and cramped compared with the main bedroom I had slept in.

THEY HAD KNOWN.

2
Tiny tear

One summer holiday was spent working as a waiter in a beautiful Scottish highland hotel overlooking a cold, calm loch with brooding scenic views stretching away to the open sea beyond. Day in, day out, I carried heavy suitcases up and down hotel stairs, served all drinks at dinner, and on days off climbed surrounding local hills, usually starting off dry and coming back wet through!

I didn't have much to do with the other hotel workers — the chambermaids and kitchen staff — not because I was the only English worker, but because I worked alone. I was young and arrogant as well having an ongoing, mostly jovial, argument with the owner of the hotel. He was a Scotsman of around forty who, when he was in a good mood — usually the result of having a fully booked hotel — would order a whisky or three for staff in the bar at the end of the evening once the guests had turned in. One subject we sparred about was the existence of God.

'There is no God,' he would say, dismissing my sentences with a downward gesture of his hand.

'Yes, there is,' I would dogmatically retort, getting comfortable on the barstool, finishing off my drink and waiting hopefully for another (free) one. 'Just because you can't see something, doesn't mean it doesn't exist.'

Pause. 'I never met your father but I know he existed because you are here!'

'You're a fool, man,' he said, smiling amiably as he was my employer. 'That's not evidence,' he said, putting his empty whisky glass down on the bar as a signal for the barmaid to re-fill, and a pause for me to consider whether it was worth (somewhat politely) haranguing him a bit more.

So it would usually go on, often past midnight, until one of us got bored or until he decided the bar was closing and sent us all to bed. Me to my basement bedroom with a worm's view of the garden, and him to his chalet where he lived with his wife and twin sons.

One day, after I had finished breakfast chores, Morag (a chambermaid) put her head round the door of the small staff dining room in the basement where I was reading the local paper with my feet up on a chair.

'Fancy helping me getting some clean sheets out of the linen room?'

'Yes okay, if you like.'

I had never been in this large utility room at the side of the hotel on the first floor overlooking a small garden.

We walked down a corridor and went up a flight of wooden stairs at the rear of the hotel mainly used by the staff. Morag opened a large, white wooden door and we went in.

Involuntarily, I shuddered and clenched my fists.

There was an atmosphere in the room, apart from the dampness that hung in the air from the airing sheets. Something definitely negative was here, but what? Where exactly? Behind me? Above me? In front of me?

My spine twitched; the backs of my legs and arms seemed to hum with an unseen energy — my eyes widened as if to see the invisible better.

Time seemed to slow…

Morag brought me back to my senses.

'That's you,' she said, briskly gathering up piles of fresh linen hanging from the wall bars. 'Put your arms out,' I was instructed, as she loaded me up with clean sheets.

The prickling of my arms and legs continued as I looked around over her shoulder as she loaded me up.

I could see that it had not always been a linen room.

In one corner, in front of a large rectangular window, there was a double sink, and next to it the footprint of presumably a cooker and somewhere nearby a fridge. The floor was green linoleum, except for a strip of faded red carpet in front of the former cooker space.

Whatever was here in this this room drew back as we prepared to exit with our bundles. Once I was over the threshold and gazing back momentarily, the room appeared as it ever was.

Morag breezed down the corridor without once looking back and I duly followed. Once I had deposited my linen bundles in an adjoining room, I was sent on my way back to the main hotel area to wait upon the great and the good as they accosted me in the lobby with drinks orders, or invited me to shift twenty kilos of suitcase up the stairs to their room in return for a few quid tip.

Meanwhile, though, I was deeply troubled with what I had experienced. But what had I encountered precisely? I couldn't say. Was it all in my mind? Unlikely, considering I had had similar experiences in the past. A mental marker was set next to it and for the time being life went on…

A week or so later, it was windy and stormy outside. I was asked to help a maid collect sheets from the room again. We bustled in, me pretending everything was fine when it wasn't, Kayleigh, the maid, chatting about nothing in particular. Stepping into the room, the mess of energy once again crept up around me as my companion quickly gathered up clean linen. There was another feeling too — a sigh, a tearfulness that was part outside and part inside my head; a sob ever so faintly heard? Inside or outside the room?

Luckily, Kayleigh seemed as eager to exit the room as me and soon I had closed the door safely behind me, following my companion out.

I heaved a sigh as I sat down on the empty bed opposite where my colleague was busy working. I had to say something.

'Is there something odd about that room?' I asked.

She carried on working.

Hadn't she heard?

I asked again.

A shout came from a room down the corridor where somebody else was working. Kayleigh immediately responded and, smiling, left me alone.

I sighed.

Some days later, I was in the staffroom breakfast lounge again on my morning break reading the paper when Megan came in with a pot of tea on a tray.

'Hiya,' I said, putting down my paper.

As there was no one else on break I decided to confront her about the room.

There was a pause.

Putting down her cup, she got up and closed the room door, sat back down, almost slumping, and lowered her voice as she spoke; me sitting opposite hanging on her words.

'Around fourteen years ago Jim — the hotel owner — had just moved into a small flat within the hotel with his wife and toddler son of about three. Everything went well as their business started to make money and, as it did, they became busier. The owner was dealing with guests while his wife looked after their son upstairs in their small flat.

One day, Jim was out. Margaret — his wife — was in the flat frying chips on the oven while her son played on the carpet. Suddenly, the phone rang in the hall corridor. She had to take it as it was one of only two phones in the whole hotel at that time.

In the split second it had taken for her to step out of the room to answer it, her son had got up, walked over to the stove and pulled the chip pan full of boiling oil down onto his head, killing him.

The grief almost destroyed them.

They coped, somehow, by working in this place and, several years later, they had two wee boys. But,' and here Morag slowly, slowly straightened up and put her elbows on the table, 'they NEVER talk about it, and neither of them have ever entered that room again.'

'The linen room,' I said.

She nodded.

'I get such sadness in that room,' I said. 'And anger, and loss.'

'Of course you do. Why do you think we ask you to come with us when we go in? Us ladies have always felt it. Now you also know why there's a sink in the room, and why there is lino on the floor. Margaret tore up the carpet in a frenzy of grief where her son died.'

I felt such a fool.

Thereafter, I steered clear of arguing with the owner and never, EVER, mentioned God. As the hotel prepared to close in late October, I waited in the car park for the bus to take me to Glasgow, and onwards home to England, with a few of the other seasonal workers. Just briefly, as he helped us all to load our cases onto the coach, our eyes met. He shook my hand and there was that narrow-eyed lingering look between us.

He knew that I knew.

Finally.

Postscript. Driving past the hotel on a trip to the highlands fifteen or so years later, I pulled into the abandoned car park and got out. The whole building was derelict and boarded up. I had no idea why, and there was no one around to ask.

I picked my way through the piles of brick and rubbish strewn around. I was drawn again to that room after all these years, walking round to the side and looking up.

There it was, on the first floor, boarded defiantly up.

I turned to go, and something caught my attention in the tall weeds at the bottom of the wall. I bent down and picked up a faded blue child's plastic rattle. I shuddered and let out a cry as a tear streamed down my cheek.

I threw the object as far away as possible in the direction of the once neat garden, long since abandoned.

Getting into my car I said a prayer for the little lost soul in the linen room, before driving hastily away.

3
Music box

'He's at it again,' I said, sipping the cheap beer I had just got from the open-all-hours corner shop.

We were sitting in the cramped ground floor back room of the terraced Victorian house that was our student lodgings. Outside the tatty wooden windowsills, snow slithered and twisted in a wintery sub-zero smash and grab.

The TV was on and we were eating, sat by the only fire in the house.

'He' was our elderly next-door neighbour. 'It' was the cumbersome Hammond Organ he kept in his back room the other side of our shared common wall. It always seemed to come out when we were gathered in the back room.

When I ventured upstairs to my freezing back room garret bedroom, there was only silence from next door. It was no exaggeration to say that icicles were quietly growing on the *inside* of my window, as I crawled into my sleeping bag during one of the coldest winters on record. With just a radio for company, I was soon asleep.

So it continued for the first few months of our tenancy of the old house, as the snow unrelentingly fell outside and the ice made the road an ice-rink. Most nights, as we sat down to eat and watch TV in the one heated room in the house, we heard the dull drone of the organ drift through the walls. We never seemed to hear a melody, or anything we recognised as music, but it didn't seem to matter. It was never loud or intrusive. Though it was just a background layering of sound from less than five feet away, there was a faraway quality about it, as if no-one was actually *playing* anything; it was an energy released from decades of life and singing and talking encased in the brickwork. Melody periodically released, suspended in time.

To look at our elderly neighbour when he was sometimes pottering in the rather neglected garden, you would not, at first glance, think him capable of playing anything as demanding as an organ which needed a foot pumping it to work. He would often buttonhole one of us if we were outside and show us a black and white passport type photo of who we took to be his wife. It made us young, boisterous students with plenty of attitude quite sad to realise that he seemed to have no one else now in his life. We were probably the only people he saw most days, either in the garden (which had a back gate we used to get into the next street and an excellent student pub), or at the front of the house passing his bay window.

One day, however, early in the second term, we came home from lectures to find an ambulance outside his house. The bitter cold precluded us from hanging around to find out what had happened, but as soon as we heard our neighbour's door slam, I opened our door into the freezing night to try and find out.

'The district nurse found him dead in bed this morning,' the ambulance man told me as he got into his vehicle.

'Really?' I said, before relaying the news to my housemates huddled behind the door. I was surprised because, for one thing, none of us knew he had a nurse visiting him — though as we were out most days it wasn't surprising our paths hadn't crossed. I was also naively surprised that someone I knew of had died. We thought the old gentleman would just go on and on, like an old soldier perhaps.

We trooped back into our house, taking in this sad news as we sat down in our back living room. No more Hammond Organ as a background to our chat and TV viewing. It seemed hard to believe as, although we had only lived in the house a few months, it had become part of our landscape.

Sometimes over the next few weeks, my ears would prick up as I sat watching TV — was that music I could hear? A tinny sound drifting in from the kitchen and back bathroom? Probably the cistern. It was as old as our late neighbour. Gradually, we got used to the silence that was the next-door property. My fellow tenant had seen a furniture van outside and workmen emptying the house, including the clunky Hammond Organ, which he said looked in danger of collapsing as it was carried in an old blanket to the van. Furniture, fittings and bags of clothes, all gone. Our landlord owned that house too, we found out, and wanted it re-tenanted as soon as possible.

I awoke one bitterly cold night in my sleeping bag wearing my bobble hat and gloves. Something had woken me, but the shadows in my tiny box room betrayed no hint of its origin. Small icicles were once again breeding inside my wooden window frame, while snowflakes eddied around in the night air outside, obviously expecting to get in and join in the fun inside my room. I listened in the stillness of the night. What was that?

Drifting through the wall was the unmistakable sound of the Hammond Organ, its wheezy sounds ebbing and flowing as if it were an unreliable radio frequency. I lay still, mouth open admitting the bitter night air. I closed it, pulled the bobble hat down my face stretching the wool down to my mouth, trying to keep out the sound from beyond the grave. I put out a hand from my sleeping bag to switch on my bedside lamp, whereupon the sound ceased. I switched on my radio and lay still in bed, the fear running up and down my limbs as I strained to hear any additional sounds. There were none, just Radio Trent whispering in the background though out my night slumbers. The light stayed on the rest of the night, and I gradually fell asleep again as dawn broke on the snowy landscape outside my creaky bedroom window.

I told none of my fellow lodgers what I had heard as we warmed ourselves with hot tea and toast before going off to lectures at the college. I told myself I needed to investigate what I had heard and, faking a headache, I told my fellow tenants to go without me and I would catch them up later. Once they had departed, I got fully dressed and, putting on my winter boots as thick snow had fallen, went into the street. It was mainly empty with people mainly having gone to work, with just a few cars parked on either side of the road.

I looked at next door's bay window, and peered through the net curtains. I could see the room was empty but the room door was closed. No one had moved in, I thought, but was the house definitely empty? Only one way to check from where I was standing. The brass letter box on the solid wooden door was tempting my curiosity.

I looked around — no one was looking.

Determining to solve the mystery, I opened the brass flap for the letters and peered inside.

Empty hall, empty back room, bare stairs, devoid of life.

The faintest of melodies from somewhere.

Was it real?

Was it in my head?

I leaned on the door with my elbow and it slowly swung open. I stood up, taken aback. The landlord must have left it unlocked when he left in hurry the previous night. We had seen his car outside and heard the clomp, clomp of his feet on the wooden stairs, before a hurried clomping exit a few minutes later.

I looked up and down the street.

No one around.

I stepped over the threshold and looked into the now bare front room, with its bright wooden floorboards and tatty old net curtains.

All was silent.

The muffled sounds of an organ started to resonate, as if coming out of the surfaces of the walls and ceilings…

I spun slowly round in the middle of the empty room,

trying to find its source. The wall, the floorboards, the ceiling, resonated like a radio signal.

Somehow, I dragged myself back to the front door and fled outside into the cold.

I turned and looked back.

The light flashed on and off in the downstairs room.

Upstairs, in the dark empty bedroom, an old man's face stared down at me…

4
My child, my child

A glorious autumn morning with the sun shining through the glass panes that framed the door that leads into the garden; it was about eight a.m. and I was sitting on my bed in my pyjamas, unwrapping my thirteenth birthday presents. My younger brother was in the next bed asleep — lazy git, on a day like this! The house slumbered too, and those therein the same.

Absorbed as I was in my presents, I became aware that the room door was open, and a tall man was standing there watching me. I was immediately surprised by the fact that, though the room was bathed in sunshine, he was in total shadow, dressed in black in what seemed like old fashioned stockings and shirt, reminiscent of a Puritan I had seen in numerous pictures.

'Who are you?' I asked, looking directly at him and not in the least afraid.

He spoke to me, or rather mumbled. I couldn't understand any of it.

'What do you want?' I sat up on my haunches, craning my head, no more than ten feet away from him.

He mumbled again, then closed the door noiselessly.

I fumbled around my bed, putting on a dressing gown and slippers, and hurried over to the door, throwing it open.

'Did you see that man?' I said breathlessly to my younger two sisters in the next bedroom, who must have seen him walk past.

'Who? We didn't see anyone,' they chorused back from their beds.

'Yes, you did. You must have,' I said back, getting annoyed with both of them.

I stood there, outside our bedroom doors, gazing down the corridor which led to our parents' room and the rest of the house. My sisters got out of bed, put on their dressing gowns and came to join me at door.

It was all very confusing.

The mysterious man was the talk of the breakfast table — or rather me telling everyone else what I had seen and my siblings looking a bit awkward. My parents dismissed my tale in an instant, and that was that according to them. Talk then turned to my presents and an upcoming visit to tea rooms in town.

The holiday in the sixteenth century rectory outside Falmouth, Cornwall, carried on as we went off in the car looking at abandoned tin mines, gazing down their holes from a safe distance with our parents policing our every move. Even cream teas in busy down town Falmouth couldn't banish the man out of my mind. Subsequent mornings saw both me and my brother awake in the bedroom around the same time waiting to see if he would put in another appearance.

Nothing.

I noticed that when we played with Jane, the rector's daughter, occasionally in the large sprawling garden, she would stop what she was doing and listen carefully when I whined that no one believed me. Well, she did live in the house. Had *she* met the strange gentleman, I wondered? I was too shy to ask her directly but could see her curiosity was piqued. Football with my sisters could wait, maybe.

A couple of days later, while us children were in the extensive rectory garden surrounded by distant hills with Falmouth a mile or so away in the valley, Jane stopped playing rounders with us, and walked over to one side of the house overgrown with ivy and brambles.

'Look,' she said, pointing at one part of the outside wall.

We strolled over. A bricked-up door could be picked out, surrounded by ivy and weeds.

'Where does that go?' I asked, my curiosity awakened.

'Nowhere now. There used to be another wing of the house over there,' she said, pointing to an expanse of garden bounded on one side by a hedge and garden wall, obviously constructed on top of an earlier wall.

'Where is it then?'

'Burned down hundreds of years ago my dad told me,' she explained.

'What happened?'

'Someone knocked over a candle in a bedroom he said. He's in the churchyard.'

'Who is?' we chorused.

'The little boy who died,' Jane said, in a quiet voice.

We had all gone quiet too, as we gazed at the old door that led nowhere.

'Only his father survived, my dad said,' Jane continued. 'Sometimes I see him walk past my door. He's not bothered about visiting me though because my dad says—'

'Jane!' her mother shouted from the back door. Jane waved goodbye and trotted off for her tea, leaving the four of us to make our way back to the guest wing of the house to find our parents. Jane's story had set us all chattering, and we carried on as we sat down for tea.

'There's no such thing as ghosts!' my dad said, getting irritated. The conversation died down and we sat and ate, the four of us thinking about Janes sad story.

The next to last day of the holiday found me alone in the graveyard on a warm afternoon, while my brother and sisters were blackberry picking with my mum. Our parents had taken us to visit churches and graveyards since we were able to walk, so me being in one seemed an entirely normal activity. The rectory was the other side of the cemetery wall so I wasn't in danger of wandering off too far. I sat on a bench just outside the church door when I saw Jane climb over the cemetery wall on the far side. It was one thing visiting cemeteries and churches, but when your dad works in one and takes care of the other it must make you a bit more aware of the world, visible and invisible, so I sensed a kindred spirit.

I waved, and she sauntered over and stood in front of me in her anorak and boots. The same age as my older sister, Lucy, I wondered what she would be like as a sister? Lucy was short-sighted, so probably wouldn't have seen anyone walk past her bedroom unless they were six inches in front of her.

'Come and see this,' Jane said, setting off down a grassy path, past overgrown graves and eroded gravestones. I followed as we passed an enormous yew tree, and stood near the cemetery wall amid lumpy turf signifying old grave sites with no gravestones.

She knelt down and cleared the grassy ferns away from an ancient gravestone with faint spiralling writing.

'What does it say?' I asked, squinting down at the eroded lettering.

'This is the boy who died in the fire,' she said, tracing out his name, young it seemed but how old was he exactly? 'His mother also died in the fire, but they buried her somewhere else.'

'It seems to be a strange place to put him, so far from the church,' I replied.

'My dad told me that the vicar couldn't bear to be reminded of his only son's death every time he went into the church, so he put him away in the corner by the wall. So sad to die so young.'

Once we were on the road home, Mum decided to tell us what she really knew about the shadowy man at the rectory. Yes, there was a ghost of a seventeenth century rector who haunted the building but wasn't seen very often and yes, deny it if your children ask, the rector advised during the initial booking by phone. Jane, apparently, was under orders not to scare us, but when she heard I had seen something, decided to share what she knew.

'He probably visited you, darling,' Mum said to me later when we had got home and were sitting in the back kitchen, 'because you are a boy, and the poor man lost his only son. His restless soul returns to the house sometimes, especially when a boy like you is staying.'

'Like me?' I asked. 'What do you mean?'

Mum sighed visibly and took my hand. 'The fire broke out on the poor boy's thirteenth birthday.'

5
Separated by the sea

There is a certain country churchyard in a little village in south Oxfordshire that is very familiar to me. I attended communion services in its small Norman church over the years while teaching English every summer at a school based in the sprawling eighteenth century house close by. On one sad occasion, I was present at the burial of a very dear friend in its peaceful leafy graveyard. Thus, whenever I was in the area subsequently, I would visit his grave, wiping the headstone clean of moss and laying daffodils in a little glass vase at its foot.

On one occasion while visiting, some restoration work was being done on the asphalt footpath that went past my late friend's grave. Thus, to get to his grave from the small car park, I was directed along a gravel path through an area of lumpy grass mounds detouring round the far side of the church.

As I took this damp detour, my downward gaze was caught by a modern grey slate headstone that seemed out of place in a burial area dating back more than two hundred years. The headstone, just off the path, was definitely twentieth century, but the memorial was to someone of an earlier time:

Lucinda Green

1870
Aged 22
Lost at sea 'Union Castle'
In loving memory

I stood and pondered what I had read.

Why would someone put up a gravestone to someone who had perished at sea nearly one hundred and fifty years ago? I was intrigued to enquire further, but time was pressing.

A few months later, I was back in the area visiting a friend and, after attending communion service, I approached the priest about the headstone as he was putting away prayer books.

'Oh yes, there is quite a story attached to that,' he replied, as we stood and chatted about mutual friends from the church and the college we had both known over the years. 'Come back to the vicarage next time you are in the area and, if I'm free, I'll tell you the story.'

A few months later, while visiting a friend at the university, I had telephoned Reverend Peter in advance to arrange a visit to him, and we had agreed on a convenient time. He greeted me at the vicarage a few miles from the church, and warmly welcomed me into his rather untidy book-strewn study — the kind of study which appealed to me.

After giving me a coffee and sitting me in a comfortable leather armchair (just the accessory for enjoying one of his books) he sat down opposite and collected his thoughts. He was dressed in an all-black cassock, and his round glasses on a cheerful face inspired me to listen carefully to what he had to say.

'The modern headstone? Yes, I put it up,' he said, 'at the landowner's request. He came to me after a service one day and told me, rather awkwardly it seemed, about, he was hesitant to say, some sort of *ghost,*' (said almost in a whisper), 'that was supposedly bothering riders and horses on the bridle path that ran past the church yard.'

I sat up straight at this point. He had my attention now — a ghost upsetting horse riders?

'Yes, well,' he continued. 'A man in Victorian clothes wearing a black top hat was repeatedly seen walking the length of the bridle path from the direction of fields further down by the river towards the church. He appeared agitated and walked as if he were in a hurry. He appeared at various times of the day and occasionally at night. The figure would reach the churchyard, enter through the lychgate, and disappear.'

'Why did he suddenly start appearing?' I asked.

'Well, no one was quite sure really,' Reverend Peter replied, 'but I came to suspect there was a connection with the farm site. It used to be situated amongst the fields next to the church, but was demolished after the last war. A few years ago, the landowner had started some building work on the site and this seemed to have disturbed whatever spirits there were lingering on the site.'

'What's this got to do with Lucinda Green, whoever she was?' I asked.

'Well, that's where the story gets strange,' Reverend Peter said, putting his coffee cup down on the small table.

'As I said, the landowner was getting complaints

from riders using the bridle path, so he decided to employ a local historian to find out if there was any information on the farm's previous tenants because the ghost seemed to be connected to it. It wasn't an easy undertaking. Where would you start? The farm had been long demolished, and records of the tenants sparse to say the least.

'Anyway,' Reverend Peter continued, 'this historian was looking through the archives of the old local newspaper going back decades, and eventually found an entry from 1870 headlined "Local Tragedy." It appeared the farmer living there then had become engaged to a girl he had met in Canada while working on a farm there. She was to join him here in England and they were to be married. Sadly, while the ship was bringing her over the Atlantic from Canada, there was a terrible storm, and the boat sank with all aboard.

'The historian also discovered that the farmer always had to come up to the main house for his post, as he was a tenant of the local landowner. His quickest route to the main house was through the churchyard. When he found out his fiancé's ship had sunk he was desperate for news and every day tore up to the main house to see if there were any letters for him.

'There has been no subsequent record in the paper of the farmer's reaction subsequently. The story ended there. However, I decided, after hearing the landowner's sad story, that this poor girl deserved a headstone as a way quietening the disturbed soul of the poor farmer and give him some peace. I asked the bishop if I could put up a gravestone for the hitherto unknown girl whose name I now knew from the historian. The parish sexton a little later erected a small headstone and I heard no more about any hauntings. I never found out where the farmer was buried, but if it was in my churchyard then I pray they are together again for eternity.'

I thanked Reverend Peter for telling me the story and for his hospitality, and so took my leave.

I drove back to the church and parked next to a war memorial outside the lych-gate. The path to the site of the farm was down the lane on my left. Sunken green mounds over the field gate behind me betrayed that I was, in fact, standing in the middle of a deserted village site — land though now empty around the church had probably been inhabited for centuries.

It was getting dark when I walked slowly for a few yards along the high bramble hedge to a clearing where the farm had stood. I looked over the gate into the field where the ghost had been witnessed — even in the evening gloom the uneven ground betrayed buried farm foundations. Perhaps disturbing the site of the old farm had indeed disturbed a restless entity still mourning his loss from so long ago.

6
Dying to believe

'That's decided then, okay?' Ronnie held onto my hand and smiled.

'Yes,' I said, chuckling, shaking his hand. 'Why not? Can't hurt.'

'Whoever dies first comes back to tell the other one there's life after death, okay?'

'Right,' I replied, and sat back in my easy chair.

We sat in a fairly tatty lobby in a Middle Eastern hotel overlooking the Red Sea. Drinking coke and making death pacts was not my normal way of spending an evening, but here we were, several of us English teachers thrown together in a down town hotel while our villa was being renovated. Ronnie, roughly twenty years older than me, had shared his previous experiences as a fellow student of the paranormal when the subject eventually came up in conversation after exhausting every other subject. We had decided such a light-hearted agreement would cause no mutual harm, and I soon forgot about the whole thing as we started to live the busy lives of well-paid expats.

Several months later, I returned home after work and was relaxing on the balcony with colleagues when Salim, our Sudanese company house manager, appeared. He had a grim expression on his face.

'Guys, I have some bad news,' he said, sitting down heavily on a vacant chair.

We switched the music off and turned to look at him.

'What's this about?' we asked.

'Your friend Ronnie… is dead.' He paused, waiting for a reaction. Silence. 'He dropped down dead in front of his students.'

'What? How?' we gasped when the power of speech returned.

Salim outlined the circumstances of Ronnie's death in the middle of an ordinary English lesson.

It was too surreal to take in. I had only been joking and drinking with him a few nights previously. He had been house-sitting a large company villa for a senior manager and his wife who were away on holiday, which was why I wasn't surprised when he hadn't come home after work.

'The company need to send all his effects to his widow,' Salim said after a long pause while we took in the shocking news, sighing with genuine sadness even though he didn't know any of us really, and never spent any time with us socially. 'Someone has to help me when I go in his room to pack up his things.'

'I'll do an inventory with you if you like,' I said later, still in shock at the loss of a friend I had got to know quite well over the past six months or so.

By the time Salim unlocked Ronnie's bedroom door, all my other colleagues had flown off on holiday and there was just me left to catch my flight the following day. Salim, myself and a couple of his assistants slowly and reverently walked into the darkened room, opened the curtains, switched on the air conditioning and started to gather up his clothes and effects, all carefully itemised and put into company cardboard boxes, ready to be shipped back to the UK.

The sum total of a person's life — albeit a life abroad as a contractor. I was especially moved by the family photograph in a silver frame and the diary opened on the table ready for a daily entry. I closed it without reading anything and brushed back a tear. We completed our solemn task in silence and with due care. Salim and his helpers loaded all the boxes into a truck parked outside and, soon after, drove away leaving an unlocked empty room so recently lived in. Ronnie was definitely gone now.

I walked back to my side of the villa by myself and put the TV on, fixed a large drink, and tried to think of something else.

Early next morning, after a restless night for me, my taxi arrived outside to take me to the airport and the plane taking me out of the country for the next three weeks, thoughts about sad events forcibly consigned to a cupboard at the back of my brain.

A late-night double rap at my hotel door.

'Who the bloody hell's that?' I whispered in an irritated voice.

I had just flopped down on the bed of the large airport hotel after a long flight back to the Middle East from the UK. It was close to midnight and, apart from the hotel receptionist and the luggage porter, no one else was around.

I got up slowly, opened the door and gazed up and down the long brightly lit corridor.

No one.

Silence.

Closing my room door, I walked back to the bed and lay down. Just as I was picking up the remote to switch on the TV there it was again.

Two quick knocks.

I got up and, somewhat brisker, walked up to the door.

Opening it, I looked out.

No one there.

Again.

Someone is playing tricks, I thought. Gently, I tried a couple of doors either side of mine. No one there. Doors locked.

I decided to wait by the door to catch the individual who must be playing tricks on me. He would get such a mouthful.

I stood inside my room by the door and waited.

I didn't have to wait very long.

Just as my mind started its late-night wandering — no mini bar — no food apart from a few biscuits — there was a muffled rap the other side of my door.

Quickly I grabbed the door handle, opened the door and gazed out.

NO ONE!

Impossible.

By now I was angry and thoroughly spooked. I started to tremble and hovered by the open door while I scrutinised the corridor in both directions.

That's it I thought. I will ask reception for another

room. I will. I went back into the room, lay on the bed fully dressed and put the TV on, my gaze continually drawn to the door.

From then on there was silence.

No more knocks.

Eventually, I drifted off to sleep in my dressed state with the TV still on in the background. Early morning found me awake, in a bad mood and getting ready to catch my connecting flight back to the oil town where I was working.

I arrived back at my villa still sullen and tired after an uneventful flight, the hot sun and my sweaty room doing nothing to lighten my mood. I put on my air conditioning and looked around before going into the living room. It was empty, apart from the large leather sofas and huge TV perched at one end of the room. Returning to my room, I started to unpack my overweight case.

Someone came in the front door and was walking up the stairs.

I put my head out. It was our house manager Salim.

Pleasantries were exchanged while the sad circumstances of our previous meeting were alluded to.

'I wonder how the funeral went?' I said to Salim, as I leaned on my bedroom door frame. 'I'll send his widow a letter.'

'They haven't had his funeral yet,' Salim replied hands on hips.

'How do you know?'

'His body is still in the country. It hasn't been given an export license yet. It's in cold storage at the airport hotel.'

7
The painting of Mrs Brightwell

It was clear enough. Mr George Davis and his group of fellow workmen had had their orders from the eighteenth-century mansion's owner, Major W. Stewart, one summer towards the end of the nineteenth century. They were to take up the rotten wooden floorboards on the ground floor corridor of the old mansion, as well as plaster and repaint the walls. The faded crockery sets housed on rickety hooks along the same corridor were to go into storage. The large, framed portraits that hung along the corridor would have to be stacked and afterwards cleaned.

Major Stewart had inherited the house after a long period of it being shut up and abandoned after his relative, a distant aunt, died. The major, living in London, had little use for the old rambling pile, mentioned as far back as Domesday, but thought he could make at least the ground floor rooms and corridor habitable. Whether any of his young family would ever want to move there in the middle of the Berkshire countryside was another matter.

As soon as Mr Davis arrived on the premises and had his instructions from the major, he started to organise his men. Two assistants gingerly started to take the old family portraits off the corridor walls and stack them in a large reception room at one end of the house looking out to the walled garden. The faded outline of paintings on cobwebby walls betrayed their antiquity and that nothing had been touched for decades.

One painting in particular caught the workers' attention; it was easily four feet by four feet of an elderly woman dressed in an eighteenth-century mourning dress. She sat in an armchair with what seemed a haughty air, the viewer's gaze drawn to her piercing eyes by the surrounding black shades of bonnet and background. She was, Major Stewart explained, Mrs Brightwell, grandmother of the last male relative, his uncle, to live in the house. The frame of her painting was heavy gilt and encrusted with layers of wax and dust, while the strings holding up her painting were decayed and worn.

Up to a dozen paintings were heaved off the dusty corridor wall and carried down to the reception room earmarked for their storage. Mrs Brightwell's painting ended up being put at the end of a group like books on a bookcase. Mr Davis's company set about cleaning and re plastering the ground floor as instructed by the major.

The main doors and windows were opened to expel decades of dust from the walls and floors. Outside, in the courtyard, new planks of dark, seasoned wood had arrived by horse and cart from a nearby small railway siding. Slowly, a pile accumulated to replace the rotten wood taken up from the old house floors. Tins of paint and varnish were also stacked in what was the old dining room next to the reception room where the paintings were being stored.

One warm day, Richard, an apprentice painter and

decorator in Mr Davis's team, was sent down to the living room to open the windows to let in the fresh air. As he set to opening the two large, square panelled windows, his attention was drawn to Mrs Brightwell's painting that was visible on top of other antique artworks. He stopped what he was doing and looked curiously at the painting, and in particular the sitter's expression. *Surely it had changed?* Did she really have that sneer on her face when he had removed her painting from the wall?

Richard tried to forget what he had seen, but as the day wore on and the work of laying a new floor continued, he decided to tell a fellow apprentice what he had seen.

Alfred, the fellow apprentice, snorted loudly in disbelief, but was persuaded to be shown what Richard had seen. During a break in work, when Mr Davis was occupied in another part of the building, the pair went down to the living room where the paintings were stacked. Mrs Brightwell's painting was sought out and closely inspected. Her expression was clearly the same as it had been the day her painting was taken off the wall. Alfred prodded Richard on the back and teased him for his story-telling, urging him to get back to work before they were both found idling about and dismissed.

Nursing a wounded sense of pride and honesty, Richard started to doubt his own senses — had old Mrs B. really sneered at him? Maybe the gloom of the curtained room had played tricks with his vision. That must have been it, he decided. He thought little more about the episode until a few days later, when Mr Davis's gang of workmen were deployed in filthy weather to mix and apply white wall plaster in readiness to entirely re-coat the whole ground floor corridor walls, a task that would easily take several days once applying the intricate cornices was considered.

Major Stewart had come up from London to supervise the operation and, as it happened, Richard was sent down to the living room where the paintings were stored, on a minor errand. Mrs Brightwell, to be honest, had slipped his mind, so in the gloom as he opened the heavy, dark oak door he knew where the tools were kept.

Habit made him glance at Mrs Brightwell's painting.

The painting was empty!

Richard stood stock-still, his mouth ready to shout, but no sound emerged.

He heard a rustling.

He looked over to the far side of the darkened room to the side door to the kitchen area.

A lightning strike outside in the grounds allowed enough light into the room — a figure in black with a wizened pale face was momentarily outlined in blue. It stood motionless, but the expression was glaring and the mourning dress was the give-away.

Mrs Brightwell.

Richard didn't know how long he watched her before he ran, but the sudden noise of boxes being kicked over, heavy items dropped on the floor and the expression on Richard's face as if the very devil was after him as he clumsily exited the room caused his comrades to come quickly down the corridor to see what the commotion was.

His story was blurted out to an incredulous audience,

and upon further inspection of the room by Major Stewart and Mr Davis, each carrying a stick, the room appeared as it always had been. There were the paintings all stored with Mrs Brightwell's painting on top — her expression as serene as ever. The major and Mr Davis looked at each other and invited the apprentices to inspect what they had found.

It was impossible, Richard thought.

Was he losing his mind?

Later, as the storm decreased and the labourers made their way back to work down the corridor, the major was assured, in the presence of the entire group, that there would be no more dramas, no more wild stories about ghosts, and the renovation work would be completed.

Soon enough, the ground floor corridor was completed with new plaster walls and a shiny new set of dark wood floorboards along the entire length. Electric lights were also installed the entire length and, leading into the hitherto shut up house lobby, its intricate marble-patterned floor was also renovated along with new window shutters. The major had decided, however, that the old family paintings were to be consigned to the attic as they would be too off-putting to his family, soon to move in. The antique crockery would suffer a similar fate.

One cold winter's morning, Mr Davis and a couple of his workmen were designated to move the offending items up to the attic at the top of the house.

No-one was looking forward to the job really. After letting themselves into the empty house, they tried to switch on the lights. Nothing happened.

The electricity was off for some reason, so they would have to work by natural daylight.

They walked down the gloomy corridor and opened the shuttered windows in the lobby to allow some outside light in.

Walking down now to the storage room where they were destined to start work, they lit paraffin lamps bought with them for just such an emergency.

They opened the heavy door and stepped in to assess the task set for them by the major.

Finding that the stack of paintings had apparently fallen off the shelf, and were lying strewn across the faded carpeted floor, unsettled the nervous group of workmen. Earthquakes, however, were not unknown even in this part of rural England and although they themselves had never felt one in their own homes it seemed the only explanation.

Putting the paraffin lamp, down on the floor, Mr Davis's men started to help pick up the paintings but, sorting through, found an empty frame.

Had someone broken into the empty house and stolen a picture? A sense of confusion gripped Mr Davis as he picked it up to see the frame wasn't empty.

The dark hued canvas was still stretched out *but the image had vanished.*

The frame dimensions immediately indicated to him whose image had vanished.

With a heavy heart and more scared than he dared show to his younger helpers, Mr Davis decided that this turn of events was more than he could deal with as an ordinary small businessman. The major would have to find someone else to finish this job.

He picked up the lamp, instructed the others to follow him, and opened the oak door back down the corridor they had come from.

Mrs Brightwell's ghost was standing half way down the hall barring their way, a bony, spectral finger pointing angrily at them.

Apprentice Richard turned, knocking his paraffin lamp to the floor where it set immediate light to the carpet.

All three fled to the far end of the reception room, away from the dreadful spectre to the side door.

It was locked.

The sound of frantic pulling on an iron door handle mingled with fearful shouts could be heard as dark smoke and sublime flames started to rise in that tinderbox of a room.

8
Night porter

The small ad in the local paper said, 'Night Porter required,' and as I was short of money after graduation from university, I applied over the phone, being told at the end of the conversation with a duty manger to report for an interview the following day.

The next day the weather was foul with heavy rain, but I braved the elements for what I thought might be good employment. Taking a bus out of Nottingham bus station, I got off at a small village bus stop next to a large golf course. The hotel building, in the mock Tudor style, was at the end of a narrow lane with high hedges on either side, a large sprawling building with a spacious car park at the front.

I walked briskly down the drive holding onto my umbrella and saw a man waiting for me outside.

'I've come about the night porter vacancy,' I said, walking up to him and proffering my hand for a handshake.

'You'll take over from me,' the man said, refusing my outstretched hand and walking back into the dark wood wainscoted lobby. Round faced, pale and somewhat overweight, he seemed well past retirement age to me.

Pardon me, I thought, but let it go. It also occurred to

me that, although morose, he wasn't wet but I was.

We walked through the hotel reception area where a couple of receptionists — obviously too busy to be bothered with me — were talking to guests. It must be this old boy's job to show me round and tell me my duties as a kind of roving interview.

We trailed round the hotel corridors upstairs, and large spacious function rooms downstairs, labelled in large notices on heavy dark wooden doors, 'Breakfast room,' 'Kitchen,' 'Living room,' along with 'Hotel lobby and Bar.' Having worked in hotels before, my semi-vacant expression and limited focus tried, and failed, to sound interested. My guide, however, made no comment to me; indeed, for a man of his weight he made surprisingly little sound as we padded round on the thick red carpets that covered the corridors upstairs.

Then, downstairs again, we stepped into a large empty room at the back of the hotel. It was furnished with a raised wooden stage at one end and circular tables covered in white table cloths that covered a dance floor that stretched to the far corners of the room.

I didn't need to be told what to think about this room.

I didn't like it, but before I had time to reflect on why my host broke in,

'This is the ballroom,' he said in a quiet voice, and led me across the parquet wooden floor to the French windows on the other side of the dance floor. 'You should know there is, what you might call, a presence here,' he affirmed, looking around furtively as we walked. 'The previous manager has been seen here,' he said, stopping and pointing vaguely. 'He had a heart attack and drowned in the swimming pool outside one day after work. They brought his body in here on a stretcher before the ambulance arrived.'

'Have you seen him?' I asked.

'No,' he said, 'but I have felt him around. I just come in, have a quick look, and leave.'

We stood by one of the glass doors covered in streams of rainwater and looked outside through the watery gloom. The pool was covered in a plastic cover, and the whole area looked a bit neglected. I turned to go, but my host seemed lost in his thoughts.

I lingered by the windows for a while, but then my guide turned to walk slowly back whence we had come.

I really wasn't happy now. There was a heavy dampness in the air; a dull electricity fizzed all over my bones.

Sighing, and with a resigned air, I followed my guide as he walked on noiselessly ahead of me out of the room.

Could I just chuck all this and go home?

As we got back in the hotel lobby area, I had made up my mind, reluctantly, to reject any job offer. As I turned, however, to thank my host after momentarily closing the door behind me, he was already gone.

'Miserable git,' I said audibly, as I collected my thoughts and wondered what I was expected to do next. He obviously couldn't wait to leave as well!

It was all a bit casual but before I could speculate further…

'Can I help you?' one of the smartly dressed hotel receptionists called over to me.

'Well,' I said walking over, 'your night porter showed

me round, and has now disappeared, without telling me if I had got the job or not?'

'*The night porter?*' the young lady replied, looking suddenly perplexed. Her pinned on hotel badge and name identity tag on her jacket lapel rose and fell as she took an involuntary deep breath.

'Yes,' I said, looking around to see if my earlier guide might put in an appearance. 'He told me about the previous manager who, er... haunts...?'

Before I got a chance to continue my ghostly allegations, the lady, who I could see was called Samantha, had motioned me to sit down on a sofa across from the reception desk and telephoned for two coffees to be provided.

And called her boss.

A few minutes later, I was sat with the duty manager with Samantha standing beside him, and me sipping strong coffee.

'This is odd,' the manager said, sitting up straight next to me. 'We have no night porter at the moment. That's why we advertised. Who did you see?'

I told him about the pale, rather overweight man who had met me, shown me round and disappeared as I came back to the lobby. 'You saw me come in,' I said to Samantha.

'Yes, but you were alone,' she said. 'I assumed you were going to the hotel bar.'

'The thing is,' the manager said to me, going a shade of white, 'we had a night porter, but *he* died of a heart attack in the swimming pool last week.'

9
Through the glass, darkly

*'All shall be well and all shall be well
And all manner of thing shall be well.'
(Mother Julian of Norwich c.1343-c.1416)*

I was asleep, but it wasn't a peaceful sleep.

Actually, I was wide awake, but not in the waking world I was familiar with.

I was standing on a dark plain with light emanating from stars far overhead, like in a planetarium I had once visited; above me and all around me, but out of arm's length, vague, white humanoid shapes danced and slithered; somewhere far away, too, I heard a melody of some kind resonating in the inky blackness.

I sensed I was in a crisis of some kind though I felt strangely calm. In my mind I could 'see' my physical body lying in darkened room on a hospital bed, covered in a white sheet; my eyes closed and my head wrapped in a bandage on a white pillow.

'Malaria has got to his brain,' a nurse said to another medic who entered the room and joined her at the end of my bed, conversing over my medical notes held in both of their hands.

'Well, we've done all we can,' replied the other. 'It is

for the medicine to bring down his high fever and bring him back. We can only pray.'

'I'm only twenty-three — too young to leave,' I said, stamping my feet on this darkling plain, alone, but somehow feeling company nearby. A thought jostled to the front of my brain — this was the 'uncertain hour before morning,' as Eliot, my hero poet had put it, when, according to him and paraphrasing, the visible and invisible worlds collide.

Anything was possible.

Make it possible for me to go back!

Back to my (then) English job in West Africa! 'Now!' a small voice in my head demanded.

Who, or what, was I talking to?

My creator?

The creator of all?

'I need to see him and tell him I'm okay,' I announced to the gloom around me. The pulsating white shapes made themselves visible in my peripheral vision, seemingly dancing with a joyous synchronised momentum.

A pause.

I could still hear a melody from somewhere.

The light under my feet began to glow dimly. Suddenly, a light from above my head shone brightly blotting out everything.

Then, as quickly as it had appeared, this light disappeared, and I found myself in the middle of a sunny garden behind a modern block of flats.

I sighed, shedding a small tear.

I knew this place.

A small boy with bright ginger hair and a toddler were playing on the grass a few paces in front of me. Over to the left in the shade there was a small pool and waterfall, round which a couple of women were sitting in deckchairs, drinking tea and watching the children play.

Feeling the gentle breeze of the afternoon on my skin, I walked towards the boy who saw me, looking up from his toys. He smiled and showed me his toy car.

I smiled back and said, 'Hello.'

'Hello,' the boy replied.

A knowing pause.

'I know who you are,' he said, slowly, 'and why you are here.'

He went back to playing.

'Don't worry,' he said, without looking up. 'You are safe.' He was barely four years old. How did he know?

'Thanks,' I replied, rooted to the spot, emotions welling up.

The toddler, a girl, then stood up next to a small sandpit and smiled at me holding her dolls.

'Jonathan!' his mother shouted over to the boy. 'Who are you talking to? Come here both of you!'

'Go,' the boy said to me and walked off holding the girl's hand. A backward glance and small wave from him at me melted my heart as I sank back into the shadows.

'Who was that man you were talking to?' I could hear his mother asking, looking over to the grassy area, which was now empty.

'Me,' the small boy confidently told his mother.

'Don't be silly, Jonathan,' his mother replied, picking up both of her young children and taking them back inside to escape the hot African sun. 'How can you talk to yourself?'

I was alone again in the flat, dark world I had come from.

What was I to do now? I heard the hospital medics again.

'The fever is still high but it seems to be coming down.'

Then they were gone, and the darkness returned.

It felt like I was waiting for something, or someone.

Just then, a boy came cheerfully towards me out of the darkness, lighting up the space around us. He had brown hair and a familiar look about him. In his hands he had a basketball.

'Hello,' I said.

'Hi,' the boy said, as he started to bounce the ball noisily on the floor.

'Do you like basketball?' I asked him.

'Yes, but not as much as playing Call of Duty,' he smiled back, with an accent I couldn't quite place.

'Really?' I said. 'What's Call of Duty?' Then, 'Wonder where you got that accent?'

'From you of course,' the boy shot back. 'So, I need you to go back and get better. I want my life too!' he said, grabbing the basketball with one hand and my wrist firmly with the other.

I fell back on the floor, open mouthed, and with a start was back in my hospital bed looking up at the ceiling, eyes wide open.

'Yes, I will get better, I promise,' I rasped as loud as my feeble lungs would allow. 'I will, I will…'

A nurse rushed into my room and checked my vital signs.

'Your fever has gone,' she said, smiling, checking my vital signs. 'Who were you talking to?'

Postscript. My half English, half Turkish son was born in Istanbul in 2008.

10
Failed to return

From out of nowhere, the low drone of a light aircraft could be heard in the gloom of the night, circling low from over to the left and then heading off over our heads in a southerly direction. As there was no moon, we couldn't see anything in the pitch blackness, only hear the whine of an engine as it throttled out at the start of its journey.

Soon the noise faded and died.

It was after midnight on a bitterly cold winter's night in December 1979. I was out with fellow Venture Scouts on a night hike as part of a Sixth Form course we were attending at school.

'Who the hell is flying on a night like this?' we wondered aloud, trying to find our way along a muddy footpath in the gloom. Our path took us past an old airfield a few miles outside Bedford; our destination being a car park on the other side of the attached village where one of our leaders was waiting with flasks of tea and sandwiches.

The path followed a decayed wire fence for much of its length and, here and there, great square slabs of eroded concrete lay end to end betraying their wartime origins. The site seemed long abandoned, had been for many years except for a working farm at one end. The only vehicles that used the concrete runways now were probably farm vehicles and combine harvesters.

In the small hours of the morning, we reached our rendezvous point and sat in the back of a warm Land Rover, too tired and cold to think about much else except getting home to a warm bed.

A few days later, and borrowing my dad's Ordinance Survey map, I took a closer look at the area we had hiked in — I hadn't chosen the route after all. When I realised, we had passed along the boundary of the old wartime airfield, I took a deep breath and put down the map and tea I was drinking. Everyone in Bedford knew the wartime bandleader Glen Miller had taken off on his final flight from the wartime airfield, disappearing over the Channel on his way to Paris. I had even seen a plaque on the wall of the Corn Exchange in the town centre commemorating his last concert there. My go-to ghost guide to the United Kingdom, Hippisley-Coxes' 'Haunted Britain,' told me all I needed to know. There was a small entry for Oakwood Airfield, telling how, on foggy nights, the ghostly noise of a small aircraft could be heard overhead before disappearing into the night.

That was what we heard.

Even the date he disappeared was mentioned: December 23rd.

The same night as our ramble.

Years later, on a day off from work, I decided to visit the old wartime airfield again, having not seen the place since my schooldays.

The heritage industry had well and truly arrived and,

on this beautiful warm day in May, the old airfield was hosting dozens of visitors, mostly parking their cars on a section of the old runway. There were tours of exhibitions in restored wartime Nissan huts, wartime military and civilian vehicles and tours round the restored air control tower.

One particular Nissan hut was dedicated to the memory of Glen Miller with memorabilia donated by US combat veterans and their families with his music — especially 'In the mood' — being piped in to add to the atmosphere. Additionally, 'Wartime cream teas and scones,' served on fold down metal tables, drew excited crowds to sit and bask in the warm sunshine, reflecting how a now peaceful location was once a place of tension and high emotion. Being interested in military buildings, vehicles and models I ambled round the restored Nissan huts labelled 'Operations Room', 'Pilots' Quarters', 'Map Room' and 'Orderly Office', surveying their authentic furniture and fittings that had probably been salvaged from far and wide between here and the USA.

My attention soon wandered to the Control Tower that stood by itself, as they invariably did, at the edge of the old runway.

I wandered over, leaving behind the main groups of visitors still taking the refreshments on sale and, with a cornet in hand, I approached the bottom of the outside metal stairs that led directly to the top of the tower. Climbing up slowly and surveying the now peaceful surrounding countryside, I couldn't help but think of the life and death dramas that had played themselves out in such a small building that had been, in its day, the most important place on the airfield. Reaching the top, I had a look at the restored light green coloured war-time machinery and its bank of Bakelite phones in the middle of the room. Faded black and white maps covered the back wall while at the other end, a heavy green telescope was positioned looking towards the runways so the personnel could see who was landing and taking off.

Visitor chatter drifted in the open windows, while overhead the sun came out. It was difficult to imagine that death and destruction were planned here or that so many lives were lost taking off from here.

I sighed deeply and started to go down the internal concrete stairs down to the first floor.

As I reached the bottom rung, I had a cursory look at the long tables that had been set out with maps and plans strewn all over them, but my attention was immediately taken by a man in a pilot's uniform who was standing outside on the balcony. He was gazing across the runway but, when he saw me, he turned and smiled.

I smiled back and waved, continuing my journey down to the ground floor.

Later, at the exit and small gift shop, I was buying a book about the history of the airfield and its connections with Glen Miller. 'I heard his plane once,' I said to the obviously long retired man in a military tie manning the till.

'It used to be a common occurrence,' he said, 'but we don't hear so many reports these days.'

'I liked your historical re-enactor in the Control Tower,' I said, picking up my souvenirs. 'Very authentic.'

The man at the till looked nonplussed. 'We don't

have any re-enactors working today,' he said quietly. He took me outside the room after leaving a colleague at the till. 'The Control Tower is haunted though, but we don't advertise it,' he said, taking me to one side to make sure we weren't overheard. 'A wartime pilot is sometimes seen standing on the first-floor balcony — we don't know who he is but, for some reason, he is drawn to the tower. Maybe the last thing he saw before he went on his last mission.'

11
Time twists

Children like certainties but when, as a child, I came to realise there were other dimensions of existence beyond the three I lived in, my natural anxiety levels, coupled with chronic asthma, conspired to periodically shake up the waking world I tried to make sense of. Two psychic strikes on my senses in particular caused me much emotional and physical pain.

In June 1975 as a shy, asthmatic thirteen year old, I joined a school trip to Hadrian's Wall in Northumberland. Having no particular thoughts about my trip beyond excitement at going on my first trip away from my parents, I set off in a coach from Bedford up the A1 to the Youth Hostel at Once Brewed a mile or so from the wall. Setting off in high spirits, and singing rude songs on the back seat, we were eventually told by our teachers to quieten down and look at the views. Toilet stops, bags of sweets and over two hundred miles meant that, by the time we arrived, we were ready to jump off the coach and straight to play football at the back of the hostel in the setting sun until supper was ready. Extreme tiredness inevitably kicked in once we had eaten, and bed was the only place we were going.

Next morning, after a lively breakfast and some

preparation for what we should find on our wall walk, we all got dressed in boots and waterproofs, ready to head down the country lane towards the crags, over which Hadrian's Wall snaked its way. Cold but sunny weather brought forth an extended crocodile of excited chatty teenagers in shiny greens, browns and greys, accompanied by several teachers at the front and back keeping watch over us.

My first sight of the ruined wall was arriving at a small gate between two steep hills with Roman wall foundations.

I paused, staring at the tumble-down walls and empty fields beyond.

It was as if a bar-code in my head had been zapped by a bar-code from beyond.

An invisible energy had me transfixed.

Images of a high stone wall from a far-off time flooded my senses — left, right, up to the parapet; men in shiny metal and leather skirts shouting at each other in a language unknown to me, almost knocking me off my feet.

I became mute, dribble eddying out of the corner of my mouth; involuntarily, I took a deep breath and held on to the upright wooden post at a set of wooden steps attached to the top of the wall.

Blinking punctured my trance and our lead teacher became visible, indicating for us to follow her up the hill path to our right, and onto the top of the crag for a better view of the ruined wall as it disappeared into the distance.

I still couldn't move.

'Come on, Jonathan, no loitering!' she shouted back,

seeing lingering at the field gate.

Everyone climbed over the gate telling me to get a move on as they trooped past.

The men in metal faded.

Once again the wall was ruinous.

I moved on, jolted out of my paralysis by a stream of classmates. On the outside, I was clambering up the hill with the group, but on the inside my head was suddenly full of anxiety — *this wall was never like that — the top part is missing — why is the wall empty now?*

Why was I bothered by these conflicting thoughts?

Hadrian's Wall had never been a topic I got upset about, but now my mind was hosting a roaring argument. But who was arguing? Me? Unlikely, surely. *'Tell someone this is not what it should look like,'* — so I told someone.

'Miss, this isn't how it should look,' I said, shaking my head to my young teacher as I caught up with her along the path.

'Don't be silly, Jonathan,' she replied over the heads of several of my companions who turned and looked at me with slightly squinted faces and eyes.

I plodded along increasingly anxious about what I could see and couldn't see as well as fending off sarcastic comments from my class mates.

'What a loony!'

'What's wrong with him?'

'But Miss, it's not fair,' I wailed quietly from the group, struggling to keep up while conducting a 360 degree observation of my surroundings.

Although my teacher admired my carefully observed

artwork she was getting a bit irritated with my odd behaviour. 'If you can't say sensible things, Jonathan, you can go to the back of the line!'

I went quiet but walked along my bottom lip quivering and clenching my fists, things I had never really done before.

We arrived at what Miss called a Mile Castle ruin attached to the wall. Everyone perched on the side of dull square foundation stones, ready to complete the assigned worksheet. Me? I sat down too but couldn't settle. What was I looking for now?

We were told to draw what we could see, so I drew the Mile Castle gate, but I had to draw it with a roof and windows and told teacher that's how it should look.

She liked my sublime shaded drawing, but wanted one of its present day look, which I reluctantly did. As the sky remained blue, we all sat and drew several wall pictures and some studied landscapes. My landscape showed the Roman road running parallel to the wall with some legionaries walking on it. We all shared our pictures later that day when we were back in a large classroom attached to the Youth Hostel. I was the only one who had drawn what Miss had called a reconstruction and attracted admiration and criticism in equal measure.

'You don't know what it was like then, do you?' someone would say to me.

My colour picture of a Roman soldier was liked by many of my classmates as much for the colour as the correct proportions of the body I had given him.

'How do you know what a Roman soldier looked like? Those colours. How do you know?' my best friend asked, looking over my should as we finished off our artwork.

I knew because I was married to one...

Postscript Many years later, during family history research, I discovered that ancestors on my mother's side had lived in Newcastle within sight of Hadrian's Wall, probably going back many generations.

***

July 1977, and I was on my first road trip up to North West Scotland, where I was due to join friends on a camping and mountain climbing trip. Being very shy, I had resisted going anywhere with anyone, and I particularly hated camping. But, after my parents bribed me with £10 and new clothes and boots, I gave in. A young family friend, Mike, had picked me up from my home in Bedford in his new car, and within half an hour we had joined the M1 and were heading up north, eventually joining the M6.

After staying the night in Carlisle Youth Hostel, we set off for Glasgow and the Scottish Highlands on an empty M6. As we started to cross the border, the sun came out and started to shine. Sitting in the passenger seat and enjoying the thrill of speed, I put on my new sunglasses and turned the hypnotic beat of Tubular Bells up.

Then, without warning, my mood changed.

Something outside my conscious world had got hold of my attention.

I became anxious, scared and even tearful.

Mike, immediately worrying at my sudden changed demeanour, pulled over the car on the hard shoulder to check me out. I wiped my nose and eyes and apologised, at a loss to explain what was wrong with me. It was a beautiful day and here I was, indescribably sad and breathing laboured breaths like I was starting to wheeze. I looked out of the all the car windows — the sky then held my attention, but I could see nothing. It reminded me of the Buddy Holly song, *Raining in my heart'*. Nothing spoilt the view, only my anxious behaviour was getting in the way.

Soon after, Mike set off in the car and, as we progressed further north towards Glasgow, my mood lightened. I seemed to recover my old chatty self, helped probably by the pie and chips Mike bought me as we sat in a motorway service centre outside Glasgow. I couldn't explain my sudden fears and it was soon forgotten as we arrived at the camp site north of the fishing village of Lochinver.

Two weeks of superb holidaying passed in meeting new friends and climbing and walking in beautiful Sutherland did wonders to overcome my withdrawn behaviour. Invariably dodging sudden rainstorms that drifted in from the Atlantic made us concerned for one another, and we thus became one interconnected group of friends.

Going home with a new sense of concern and sympathy for my fellow man, we drove back down the A9 stopping at Strathpeffer Youth Hostel for a chance to visit the sinister Loch Ness, though without seeing anything monsterly. The next day, on the M74 South to the English border, the same emotional turmoil was visited upon me again, seemingly out of nowhere.

Again I was agitated, sniffing back tears; again I was gazing all around the outside of the car looking for a source of this fear. The sky repeatedly forced my attention, but yet again it was bright and sunny with wispy clouds high up in the atmosphere.

Mike asked me if I wanted to stop? I said no, keep going. We sped on down the motorway and we disappeared over the English border.

Just then, I turned to see the name of the town named on the exit junction of the large blue motorway sign on the north bound carriageway from whose direction we had just come.

Lockerbie.

12
Genius Loci

'High school building work collapses! Again! Genius Loci blamed!'

Thus ran the hysterical local newspaper headline in the town in Southern England where I started attending private school in my early teens. I arrived in the September to find builders shoring up the floors in two areas of the main complex of school buildings at the top of the hill facing the main road at the bottom.

I saw the collapsed tile floors as well as the back wall of the sports hall at the bottom of the hill also cordoned off to be rebuilt. Who, however, were the *Genius Loci?* As I was now studying Latin O Level, the allusion in the local rag's tag-line, *Genius Loci*, our Latin Master explained to us, was to spirits believed by the ancients to inhabit natural places such as trees and rivers. And yes, hilltops too such as the one where our school was now situated. Apparently, these protective entities had, in bygone times, been placated with gifts of food and wine, and even the odd human sacrifice in order to behave peacefully towards the world of man. Memory of such entities had survived into modern times and, in particular, in connection to our school site. It was said they were displeased with what man, in particular the local authority, had done to their beautiful hilltop with extensive views across the county from the back of the school and over the cricket fields and town beyond, from the front.

'Dig out the old newspaper reports in the school archives, boys,' our Master intoned to us during a lesson on Pliny. 'The old house on this site was cursed, evidently,' he said, then pausing for effect. He then furtively looked around his desk as if it were about to be swallowed up by the spirits.

I was intrigued by the newspaper headline and, as a member of the school local history club, I had access to the school archives kept in a small office at County Hall in the town centre. Friday afternoons usually found me there assisting the school archivist — then a boy in his last year at school — in indexing and sorting related school documents and compiling interesting pieces for the school magazine. The archivist was keen that I could investigate the history of the school site so I was directed to bulging files labelled 'School site before 1974,' (the date when the school was built).

What had my Latin Master meant when he told us the school site was still inhabited by earth spirits of some kind? Newspaper reports, apart from dramatic headlines about spirits knocking down school walls, also talked about corruption in a local construction company, resulting in shoddy building methods leading to floors and walls collapsing soon after construction. The report also carried a couple of interviews of old people who had known the school site in earlier years and mentioning the folklore of local spirits. Without giving more details, the report also mentioned a tragedy in the house known as Moat House that had stood on the site until the 1930s. I sifted through wartime reports and plans of an Anti-Aircraft Battery stationed there, but didn't find much else until I chanced upon another newspaper report from roughly fifty years previously entitled, 'Suspected murder victim at Moat House unearthed during demolition.'

Now I was interested. Everyone at school vaguely knew there had been a previous house on the site — indeed remains of an old Victorian wall, probably a basement, had been incorporated into a large asphalted area currently used as a car park overlooking the main road that ran past the school. The newspaper report said that during demolition of the house a skeleton had been found in the basement floor with a knife in its ribs. It transpired that a female servant had gone missing many years previously in connection with a love affair and had never been found. Whether anyone was ever caught in connection with such an old murder the newspaper didn't say. I suspected the story had metaphorically died too.

The school site had certainly seen a lot of human activity in recent years but was it really connected to diabolical handiwork of displeased Genius Loci? Coincidence?

My Latin Master didn't think so. I couldn't find any more reference in the school archive to our invisible local friends so, after writing a small report for the school magazine and showing it to the satisfaction of the archivist, I put the file back and let the matter drop.

I had cause to later wonder if our invisible friends on

the hill had done the same thing a few weeks later. When there were no cars parked on the flattened asphalt area on the side of the hill, it was used as a football pitch during PE lessons. There I was, one day, running down the wall side of the pitch about to cross the ball into the penalty area when something, I knew not what, caused me to stumble and crash into the faded paintwork of the Victorian basement wall. I hit my head and bruised it on the brickwork, resulting in me in stumbling off to the changing rooms and the first aid kit kept there. I shook my head all the way down to the changing room, angrily shouting that there was nothing for me to trip over; it was as if a malicious invisible something had stuck out their malicious invisible leg to deliberately trip me up!

13
Dollies

Ian's grandmother had owned a large collection of dolls assembled, he was told, since she was a young girl. They were displayed in two large wooden display cases in her living room opposite a full length mirror. This gave the impression that much of the back room in their large detached house, and all that was in it, was twice the size. On special occasions, usually on Sundays after dinner, the grandchildren were invited to inspect the collection with his grandmother as the enthusiastic guide, picking up and pointing to endless small dressed up girls made of plastic, wood and ceramic; all dressed in a myriad of clothes and patterns.

Ian had never liked going into that room or spending time in the wretched dolls' company. There was something sinister, he thought, about the dead eyes that scrutinised him, so he tried not to linger, looking at them sideways so not as to offend his adoring grandmother's gaze. The large mirror opposite also filled him with anxiety. He didn't like mirrors anyway and covered up any he found where he lived. It was hard to explain why but something about reflections, and what might be consciously or unconsciously reflected in them, was enough to avoid them.

In time Ian's grandmother passed away and her collection of dolls was split up among several of her grand-daughters; being a boy, he didn't have to worry about inheriting any of the awful dolls but got a beautiful painting instead. His younger sister, Eileen, wasn't so lucky and inherited a dozen or so of the dolls. She quickly decided, however, that she didn't want them on display in her house, so they were banished to the attic to reside in a tatty cardboard box.

Soon afterwards she began to hear noises coming from the attic in the small hours.

'What can you hear?' Ian asked her on the phone one day.

'It sounded like tapping sounds, but it was weird kind of tapping.'

'Why?'

'It sounded almost like a code,' she said. 'And something else.'

'What?'

'It sounded a bit like there were *voices* up there, I swear.'

'I sent Jeremy (her husband) up the ladder the next day,' she continued, 'into the loft, and he found the dolls were out of their cardboard residence, finding one almost by the loft hatch.'

Ian didn't know what to make of Eileen's story but had no reason to doubt what she said. Her husband put the dolls back in the box with the lid on and left it at that.

A few nights later, they heard the same noises again. The following day, her husband went back up and found the dolls out of their box again, and this time all twelve of them were grouped round the loft hatch. This scared Eileen so much that she told her husband to get rid of them, so he packed them up and took them to a local charity shop.

She had a thought and telephoned her two cousins who had also been left dolls in their late grandmother's will. Was she really surprised by what one cousin, Alexis, told her? She too had had a similar experience, although having put them on display in her living room she awoke one morning to find them all on the floor in a heap. Being unmarried, and so shaken by the experience, she had put them in a cardboard box and taken them to the local landfill site there and then. Her other cousin, Catherine, had not taken them out of the suitcase they came in and had left them on a shelf in the garage.

There the whole story should have ended except, a few weeks later, Eileen came home late one night and the house was in darkness. Getting out of her car and holding several bags, she struggled to open the front door in the darkness and switch the hall light on.

Being worn out, she soon went to bed alone and was sound asleep.

In the small hours something woke her in the darkened room.

She turned over and there was one of the damned dolls again except…

This one was a six-foot tall embroidered doll, standing over her bed with its puffy sewn arms reaching out towards her neck.

Her scream could be heard at the end of the street.

14
The bone house

The former abbey in the Czech Republic was one enormous Ossuary — or bone house as it was referred to by the leaflet left in our hotel. It was a large white wooden building, the size of an average church, with a large underground repository for dismembered skeletons numbering up to seventy thousand.

I hadn't really wanted to visit it during a stay with my future wife in Prague for a winter holiday weekend. I knew enough about things beyond our waking world to know when to leave well alone so, when the coach pulled into the Abbey car park, I decided to get off last. Everyone else on the tour could go and view the bony contents, but not me.

Even the arch of the main door was formed out of extended leg bones and dismembered smaller ones as in-fill.

The tour guide began his speech in good English, and slowly the group disappeared into the main complex.

I hung about the front entrance and peered in. The sign said in big letters,

'NO PHOTOGRAPHS — POSTCARDS ONLY'

I wasn't ready for what I felt next.

Out of nowhere, an enormous surge of energy struck me on the chest, almost knocking me off my feet.

Shocked and open-mouthed, I rocked on my feet before retreating to the car park, hopefully out of range from further malign activity while I took stock.

The whole building was 'alive' but was anyone else as sensitive as me feeling it too?

As I was the only one in the car park on a cold winter's morning with the rest of the tour still inside, it seemed the answer was no. The weather was very cold and I didn't fancy waiting long for them all to re-emerge, but what to do?

About half an hour later, the tour group emerged from the depths of the Abbey, one or two clutching post cards and other small souvenirs. No one was snapping so I assumed they had all abided by the rules. Everyone had enjoyed their visit to this accumulation of angry anima, though God knows why?

The next few nights, however, I endured several strange dreams. I saw large groups of people and soldiers in some kind of tumult. Was it a battle? There were horses too, charging up and down fields covered in strung out ragged groups either running towards me or running away. I couldn't tell, as I was unable to understand what any of them were saying.

I became progressively more irritable at breakfast in the hotel to the dismay of my companion, who was completely unaffected. I couldn't think straight or find any more to interest me in our holiday to Prague which was coming to an end.

On the last day of the holiday, as our tour group went to a lakeside restaurant with stunning views of the mountains in the background, I asked my companion for my digital camera back so I could take some souvenir shots.

As I switched on the screen I was shocked by what I saw.

There was shot after shot of the interior of the bone house with whole skeletons incorporated into its walls and benches.

I was shocked and pointed out to her what she had photographed. She seemed nonplussed about it all.

'Don't you remember the notice telling you not to take pictures?' I asked her.

'I didn't think anyone would mind,' she replied, with a shrug of the shoulders.

'Well someone, or *something*, has minded,' I said angrily, as I started to delete the stored images. My companion loudly complained as the images disappeared but I was set in my mind. I then took multiple rural shots for my camera in an attempt to erase the hideous pictures previously residing on my camera.

As soon as the bone pictures had gone, my nightly mood lifted. I could sleep again and had no more nightmares.

I subsequently researched the history of the Abbey online and discovered that many of the bones and skeletons deposited there came from the battlefields of the Thirty Years war fought during the years 1618-1648. Some of these battles were even fought in the vicinity of the Abbey. Not only were there military casualties, but also women and children were interred there, gathered up from conflicts all over Bohemia. Most human bones ended up dismembered by the time they reached their final place of rest from a conflict likened by many historians to a proto 'first world war.' Well, much as I prayed for their souls' salvation, I didn't want any of them inside my head.

15
Risely's weird sister

A normal summer's afternoon on a lonely road in rural England.

Complete sunny silence.

Just a slight breeze in the branches of some tall trees round a bend in the road.

Suddenly, a car appears, careering all over the road, swerving away from both edges to avoid ploughing into a roadside ditch; the driver frantically looking in his mirror to see an unearthly entity chasing him, coming closer and closer…

A sparkling cloud seems to wreath the flying hellish hag powering towards him, dressed in flowing black with a long pointed hat and bony hands clutching what seems to be a broomstick.

Manic laughter penetrates the driver's car as he tries to follow the winding road and escape — why wasn't there anyone else on the road at this time of day?

Closer and closer it surged, even though the driver was speeding up.

A road junction not far ahead leading to the main road — safety at last he thinks!

One last check of his rear view mirror.

The entity was now *inside* his car — *on* his back seat;

chapped and bony hands reach and grab his neck, pulling him into the passenger's seat.

A passing farmer on his tractor found the car smashed into a ditch, doors open and the driver pushed halfway into the back seat.

The local paper was quick to put a dramatic twist on the story considering where the car was found; a notorious stretch of road considered haunted by an old woman dressed in black, riding a broomstick.

In this day and age?

Well, the legend did say there had been a gallows on the road once, and this 'weird sister' — as Shakespeare had referred to such beings in *Macbeth* — had been hanged on it. She had been accused of spoiling local farmers' crops and making the cattle lame. In previous centuries, when most people lived on the land and crop failures were common, it was not hard to find suitable scapegoats, especially old women who lived alone. On the gallows tree, she cursed the road and supposedly said they had not seen the last of her.

Thus, down the years the legend bubbled away, never entirely disappearing, even into the twentieth century. People living locally of course probably ignored such rubbish, refusing to let it put them off living and working in those same rural villages. Many local people did, however, nail a horse shoe into a wall somewhere on their property, to ward off the evil eye it was said. The farmer who found the poor deceased driver even had one secured to a heavy metal mudguard at the back of his tractor.

The cause of death was eventually reported in the paper as being trauma injuries caused by sudden impact, the usual wording put in car crash victims' death certificates.

What was certainly not reported was the curious fact that all over the back of the dead man's neck there were deep scratches and what seemed like bite marks.

16
Father Antonio

The man stumbled and fell as he ran down the muddy, gravelly village footpath late one night. Getting up again, he lurched onwards towards the safety of the Priests' Mission House in the village.

Behind him he heard a growl, but it wasn't one he'd heard before. The terror in the man's eyes meant it was a growl he needed to avoid to stay alive.

He lurched into wayside bushes in his haste to escape; his black cassock shredded by thorns and path gravel.

Getting up again, he saw the path climb ahead slightly as the first mud and plaster village houses came into view. Safe at last!

He turned his head to see if there was anything else on the path behind him.

There was, but what it was he couldn't tell.

A cumbersome black cloud didn't so much glide as clamber towards him faster than the priest could escape.

He reached the top of the path seeing the few paraffin lamps shining in the barred windows of village houses — huddled, terrified faces here and there watching the unfolding tragedy.

'Non!' the priest shouted, as he turned and faced the

menace with his arms outstretched.

With a loud cry the amorphous lumpy mass enveloped him and, very quickly, he and it sank into the surrounding rice paddy fields, leaving a trail of vapour and bubbles in the infected air.

'That's what happened to Father Antonio,' Father Brian said, finishing up, sitting up and refilling my glass with a generous gargle of bourbon.

A pause.

'My God,' was all I could slowly articulate.

'Every so often, on foggy nights, the last part of the chase is played out on the footpath to your house I might add,' he said, scratching his head and checking the air conditioning was doing its job at keeping the mosquitoes and other insect life that meant us harm at bay. 'I've never seen him but I don't go on that path much.'

Another pause.

'I wouldn't worry that much,' Father Brian thought he ought to add. 'It's just a story!'

Easy for Father Brian to say that I thought, as I later walked back to my concrete bungalow down the path that Father Antonio had fled along all those decades ago.

All I had for company along the way were the endless bullfrogs that croaked in the rice paddies from dawn till dusk. I headed out of the village toward the bush paths that led into the surrounding forests, but my house being the property of the Mission Order that employed me meant it was a prominent landmark as well as well built and maintained.

I reached home without meeting anyone dead or undead and was soon in my wooden cot bed with an extensive mosquito net covering it and asleep.

Teaching English in a Catholic Mission school in West Africa and working for an important Irish Missionary order of priests meant I had a relatively privileged life and plenty of free time. I was a few months into my two year contract before I heard whisperings that the Europeans hadn't always lived a fairly easy going life. The local people, while having long ago officially embraced Catholicism, had still, unofficially in part, adhered to their indigenous religious beliefs and practises. A local person from the Paramount Chief downwards saw no contradiction, apparently, in attending Mass on Sundays and then taking part in their own African religious practices the same day if they so wished.

It seemed, though, when the first European Missionaries came this way at the turn of the nineteenth century, they were content to adopt pretty much a *laissez faire* attitude to religion, knowing that the best policy for the success of British Imperialism was to let both traditions co-exist — and so they did, in the main.

Father Antonio, though, was one cleric who had been unhappy with this mostly peaceful coexistence. However, beyond Father Brian telling me the priest's name, the Mission Station had absolutely no records of him or even any existing photos from the time. Father Antonio had, apparently, been expunged from the history of the Church in the village I worked in. It was only a few weeks later from Doug, an American Peace Corps education volunteer and drinking buddy of the father, that I heard the strange story as it had been told to him.

Father Antonio had, apparently, decided that the African tradition of forest 'secret societies' were an abomination to his Catholic beliefs. These animistic ideas had to go. Full of the Christian proselytising energy that swept Africa in the late nineteenth century, Father Antonio was no different from any other missionary that crossed the continent from the Mediterranean coast in the north to Cape Horn in the south. These Christian folk, built schools, hospitals and, most importantly, churches of whatever denomination they hailed from and, little by little, traditional African beliefs were side-lined — local people began to be integrated into what the Missionaries were quite sure was a civilised religion and, in particular, Catholicism in this part of the country. Father Antonio decided, however, that such integration and education as to the ways of civilisation was not going fast enough and wished to speed up the process.

'Well, what happened?' I questioned Doug as we both sat on his concrete patio outside his bungalow opposite the Mission school where we both worked; him being a sports teacher, me teaching English. Doug shifted uncomfortably in his seat, seemingly unsure how to proceed.

'Father Brian was a bit vague and I don't want to add anything he didn't tell me,' he said, nervously. 'It's still an embarrassing episode for the Order, even today.'

'Why? Have they got long memories?'

'So it seems. Father Antonio was warned not to get involved with secret societies that meet in the surrounding forests, well away from the European settlers, and usually at night. Apparently, he thought that if he took a bible with him, he would be able to berate the local people he found at any heathen ceremony.'

I was captivated by the story, so when Doug stopped to get more cold beer I sat up in my seat looking around the bushy school perimeter for any signs of life until he had sat down again.

'Father Brian told me that Father Antonio decided to follow his house boy into the forest one night. His fellow priests at the Mission station tried to talk him out of going but he wouldn't listen. He was last seen walking slowly down the muddy lane through the village, his black cassock soon mixing in with the evening gloom.'

'Didn't the house boy know he was being followed?' I asked somewhat incredulously.

'Of course he did,' Doug shot back. 'Locals here know all about things that we *foreigners* don't. This guy just carried on walking towards the forest and was gone. His colleagues became very worried after an hour or two when he hadn't returned so went out with paraffin lamps along the bush paths to try and find him. They had to watch out for snakes and other shit out on the path in the dark like we do! Anyway, Father Antonio's hat was found at the top of the bush path where it reached the village, where you live you know?' he said pointing at me with his half-drunk beer. 'They never found his body, though.'

'My God,' I said sitting up, and noticing my beer bottle was empty already.

'Well,' Doug continued talking, as he went back into his kitchen to an enormous fridge you could safely stash a small brewery in, 'the result was the British authorities were persuaded not to investigate further by the local

Paramount Chiefs of the area. The Chiefs later built a large concrete Catholic Church as a way of apology; had furnished and painted it white. They also rebuilt the Catholic Mission station at their own expense on a new site outside the village near the main road, to the far away capital city on the coast. The British, however, did ban secret societies in the area of the village, and that's where the story ended.'

'Except for the father's frantic spirit forever running down the bush path,' I said, slowly, and sighing to myself.

Later, as I walked slowly home, I reflected on my own attempt to do good works in West African classrooms nearly a century later. Converting anyone to anything was definitely last on my list — survive the wildlife and climate were my priorities; anyone who learns anything from my classroom lessons was a bonus.

I picked up the paraffin lamp left for me on my balcony by my house boy, opened my front door and went in.

If only Father Antonio had had a similar agenda.

In the background, somewhere, a dull roar resonated.

17
The Indian Bedroom

The Indian Bedroom was the name of a large first floor room in a rambling sixteenth century mansion in Sussex where I worked in as an English teacher for a summer season. By the time I worked there in the 80s it was no longer a bedroom; a full-size pool table had been put in the middle of it with a couple of large sofas around the sides, and it had become one big social area.

The alcove area at one end of the room, where a bed obviously had been, was now a large storage space for text books. Cardboard boxes also now obscured the rural views from its eighteenth-century windows that stretched from floor to cornice.

This room held two mysteries for me; one being the derivation of its name, the other the origin of its particularly unsettling atmosphere. I had experienced this from the first time I went into the room, which ominously hadn't dissipated for me even when the room was crowded with foreign language students playing pool while attending residential English courses during the summer months.

On sunny days, extensive views of the countryside beyond the rectangular glass windows that stretched from the carpet to the intricate white plastered cornice ceiling drenched the room in glorious sunshine. However, even on days like this I encountered persistent chills; a growing uneasiness that slowly moved along your limbs; an anxiety that meant whenever I had to retrieve school books stored in the alcove, I wedged the bedroom door open with the fire hydrant so I could always see my way of escape. Whatever this negative energy was it never ventured beyond the room, so I was able to walk past without a care for my sanity or safety.

On one occasion, a staff member, who ran an informal late night teachers' bar in the common room downstairs, had brought some empty beer glasses to wash in the Indian Bedroom's sink unit which was situated in a small alcove down a flight of several stairs. A complete sceptic to anything paranormal, he had brought the glasses on a tray and, after having washed them, turned to leave when, in his words, it felt like he had walked into a 'fridge.' He somehow collected his balance, made it clumsily up the wooden stairs, and hared across the room round the pool table and out of the door miraculously without breaking a single glass. He could not be induced to return alone to that room. Beer glasses were washed in the ground floor toilets from then on.

A few weeks later, while the foreign language students were still in residence, a local history society were conducting a guided tour of the area and had arranged a short tour of the inside of the house. Using Niklaus Pevsner's guidebook as a source, they had previously visited the small Norman church next door and moved on to the historic house, pointing out interesting architectural aspects of the site inhabited for a thousand years or more. Climbing up to the first-floor landing on an eighteenth-century oak staircase with interesting filigree ironwork on the banisters, they assembled outside what had been the Indian Bedroom, ready to appreciate stunning rural views from its windows.

That was odd.

The key the guide was given to the room didn't fit.

Actually, it did, but something was stopping it turning.

And someone could be heard pacing in the room.

The bemused group lingered on the creaky wooden floorboards while the guide went to find the college bursar, who arrived a little later, somewhat irritated. Couldn't these wretched people look after themselves without involving him?

He tried the door again and it opened without any problem.

No one was walking inside.

The room was empty.

The tour continued without incident leaving all with unresolved questions concerning why it was the door had seemed locked and who was inside?

The following summer, a previous college employee came to present a history of the house after having done some research in the county archives. He had heard about the previous summer's incident with the tour group and the Indian Bedroom. Those of us employees who were interested in the history of the house assembled one evening, at the end of the summer school, in the spacious living room on the ground floor where the talk was due to take place. The house was now empty of students with just the staff left to put away books and tidy classrooms before locking up the following day.

Peter, the speaker, had also brought some interesting handouts for us. These included a black and white A3 photocopy of a Country Life article about the house from 1923, when it had been occupied by the family who had previously owned it.

What a gold mine the article was for people like me, interested in the house's history. There were plans of the ground floor and first floor, and there was the Indian Bedroom! The text informed us that it was named because of furniture and fittings brought back from the sub-continent by the house's owner after serving in the army there for a time there in the mid-nineteenth century. Accompanying photos showed the lavish Indian carpets and furnishings that had once adorned the room.

Peter, utilising unpublished memoirs and other county history sources, informed us that the retired colonel had been proud of his Indian possessions, particularly of the grand four poster bed that had stood in the alcove along with several large wardrobes and a thick shag pile carpet. He had lived a long life and was, it turned out, buried in the local churchyard. Peter also explained during the talk that there was nothing tragic connected with his life. After the colonel's son's death, the house was sold in the 1930s and its contents scattered into other country house collections.

We also heard about the soldiers who convalesced in the house during the last war, and their reputation of leaving such places in various states of disrepair. Then, in the '50s, the house was empty before one wing was converted into small apartments, but not apparently the Indian Bedroom.

Peter generously gave copies of all the relevant documents to the assembled group at the end of his talk and we finished off the evening with plenty of convivial drink and food.

I went away from the talk and the house feeling sadness for the shade of the last owner's father and decided the next time I was in the room, being a practising Christian, to say a small prayer and bless the room.

The following summer I was back and carried out my task, although I didn't make any attempt to spend any more time in the room. Subsequently, I heard no more reports of any strange occurrences. Perhaps the spirit was now at peace and reconciled with how the house and his old room were used, now stripped of furniture and fittings he had known in his lifetime. Hopefully, he realised that the new owners of the house had only its welfare at heart and wouldn't have wanted to do anything to sully its memory.

18
Scullery spirit

The first time anyone encountered anything odd in the scullery was on a Friday night one summer. Foreign language students studying English and residing at a sprawling sixteenth century country house were dancing away at an improvised disco held in the art room annexe to a modern teaching block. Extra plastic cups were needed to pour out juice for the hundred or so sweaty swingers so an activity assistant, Carrie, was dispatched to the kitchen to collect a tray full.

Night had now fallen and the party was in full swing.

Carrie had been gone a while and the lines of lively students were waiting in ragged lines for refreshment. Mike, the activity leader, then went to find her in some irritation; it was not a difficult task after all.

He found her sitting on the stone steps overlooking the back garden, tray next to her on the step, herself sitting still looking shocked.

'Where have you been Carrie? We're waiting for you. We're—' he stopped, realising she was in some distress. 'What's the matter?' he said, sitting down next to her, irritation now swapped for concern.

'That guy,' she said. 'Chopping vegetables. He smiled, then…'

The story tumbled out.

Carrie had gone into the main kitchen and saw a young man dressed in chef whites calmly chopping vegetables on a chopping board the other side of the large glass internal window in the main working area. She knew they were vegetables because he held up a potato to wave to her, smiling.

She was surprised.

She didn't know anyone was working in the kitchen that late, but thought nothing of it.

She momentarily picked up the plastic cups off the metal shelves and stacked a wooden tray.

She turned to wave goodbye and stopped in her tracks.

The light was off in the small room the other side of the glass and the chef was gone.

She trembled, a surge of energy twitched all over her.

Shaking still, she grabbed the tray and walked out without switching off the main lights, into the walled garden towards the annexe, but only made it as far as the stone stairs, where Mike found her. He was intrigued, but hid his own shock at such a bizarre story. Sending Carrie on her way and not fearing anything dead or undead, he walked back to the kitchen, the lights still on, and looked round.

All was still.

No one was in view.

After a while trying a couple of locked doors, he switched the light off, closed the back door and went back to the disco area.

Carrie's experience was quietly shared with fellow

staff but not the students. It was only the following year I realised my particular connection to this haunting.

That summer an English teacher called Robert worked at the college and had stayed behind one Saturday when the entire staff and students can gone to London to see the sights.

Alone as he thought he was in the building one fine day, he was ambling down to the staffroom at the far end of the house next to the kitchen. Being fond of food, he then decided to go into the kitchen in search of any packed lunches left behind by the coach staff from what they had earlier loaded onto the tour bus. The main catering staff would clock on sometime in the afternoon ready to prepare the students' evening meals, so Robert was not surprised to find company in the kitchen.

A chef, dressed in whites, was standing in the annexe. Robert passed by on his way to the main kitchen area.

Both acknowledged each other. Was that a potato he waved?

No words were exchanged so, as soon as Robert found a packet of crisps, he turned and made his way back to the staff room. He smiled at the chef as he left.

Surely, Robert then thought, there might be more crisps where he had found some and, deciding the chef had put him off, returned to the kitchen for more.

The room was completely empty and silent.

The chef had disappeared.

Robert was temporarily stunned and looked anxiously around.

A coldness took hold of him.

Feeling that not all was as it should be, he

subsequently retreated to the opposite end of the mansion and thence into a small seating area where he sat until the coaches returned from London.

The staff were again abuzz with Robert's cautiously related story, particularly as it followed on from Carrie's experience the previous year. Hamilton, the course director, seemingly took the encounter in his stride, but underneath was troubled. A complete sceptic, he did, however, speak to all the staff the following Monday morning during a staff meeting, not telling them to disbelieve Robert's experience; how could he? He did, however, tell the staff, for their own peace of mind, not to go alone to the kitchen out of hours. He also took me aside, as his deputy course director, into the walled garden for a coffee and chat when all the teachers had gone to class.

He had a colour photo with him.

We sat down on grey wooden benches at a wooden table.

He sighed.

'You remember this guy?' he said, pointing at a young man in a group of college staff standing almost on the very spot we were sitting at, more than twenty years previously.

'Vaguely,' I said, squinting.

'Yes, you do,' he said, moving the picture closer as if that helped comprehension. 'He was a chef when you first worked here. He played volleyball with you.'

I looked at the photo doubtfully. I had played lots of sports, drunk lots of beer with lots of people in those days including you, I thought.

'Anyway,' he continued. 'I can't remember if you found out after you had gone abroad to work that there had been a death here. This guy was chopping vegetables one day by himself and apparently had a seizure. He was found on the floor, dead, by his fellow workers.'

'Why didn't you tell me?'

'I probably forgot,' he admitted. 'So many people came and went working here in those days.' He paused. 'He's been seen by several people who work here full time as well as Carrie and Robert. No, I haven't seen him,' he said anticipating my next question. 'People in the kitchen just get on with their jobs and try not to think about it.'

The undercurrents of shock and wonder slowly calmed down, the college continued with the summer courses, and there the matter rested for the time being.

Approximately ten years later, towards the end of my time working at the college, the old kitchen was entirely ripped out and re-modelled. Hamilton told me an outside contracting company had come in with no knowledge of the chef who eternally chopped vegetables and, as far as I heard, once the new plan was finished, he was seen no more; the annexe had gone and the sink had gone, incorporated into a big new open kitchen area.

One small strange experience occurred the first day the staff clocked on to cook breakfast for the college staff and students in the new kitchen. The new head chef, unlocking the door into his new office, created at the back of what had been part of the old kitchen, had found on his desk an old chef's hat.

It hadn't been there the night before.

19
Guardian

I sat uncertainly in my car's driver's seat and rested my arms on the top of the steering wheel.

What had I seen the previous night?

Did I dream it?

Several long sighs later, I switched on the car engine and pulled out of the parking space outside my flat and set off to see my brother in Scotland as I had previously planned. Trying to keep my eyes on the road was difficult. I fidgeted in the driver's seat scanning the road and verges alongside as if an answer would come blowing in on a piece of paper and attach itself to the windscreen. Joining the motorway on my trip, I accelerated away as if the faster I drove, the quicker the vision would diminish in my mind.

3a.m. — earlier that morning — awake and sitting up alone in bed reading with a bedside lamp on.

Out of a darkened ceiling a large white horizontal figure, in the profile of an angel at prayer, floated down before disappearing into the floor in front of my bed, leaving a sparkling trail in its wake.

My arms dropped to my sides, the book sliding out of my hands; I sat open mouthed from the enormous vision I had witnessed; the figure, easily seven feet long, had descended like a leaf caught on a gentle breeze, hands together in the posture of prayer.

The small apartment room then reverted back to semi darkness, the eerie silence broken only by the low chatter of a radio on the parquet floor next to my bed.

After what seemed an age, I had sprung out of bed, put on my dressing gown and turned on the room light. Looking carefully at the floor hadn't helped me understand what I had seen but then, slumping in my bedside chair, my gaze focused on the spot where 'it' had appeared from out of the artex ceiling.

I spent the rest of the night on my living room sofa, turning over this visitation in my mind.

It hadn't looked at me at all — just a momentary manifestation of a presence and, as events turned out subsequently, an eternal one.

Five or six long hours later, I was on the A9 outside Perth. I decided then to have a rest stop in the vicinity. Finding a good place was easier said than done, however, as my road map was on the passenger seat so it was difficult to work out a good place to pull over.

I decided to take the next northerly exit and headed down a steep road opposite a thickly wooded hill and railway viaduct that looked disused. The road ahead turned to the left but seemed to fork at the same time.

I was momentarily confused.

Which lane was I in?

Still doing about forty miles an hour, I drove round to the left and stopped at a junction. I was the only car as far as I could see.

I looked left quickly then pulled out.

Then I realised the danger I was in.

An enormous roar rapidly approached from somewhere on my right.

Oh my God!

I hadn't looked there!

Within a few seconds a large articulated lorry had driven *right through me.* I panicked, yelled and lost control of the car, crashing onto the grass verge with a jerky crunch as I yanked the handbrake on. I shouted and cried as my body shook from the sudden stop.

I looked up.

The lorry had disappeared.

Completely.

Impossible.

I switched the engine off shedding angry tears but, in my shock, remembering to feel relief at having somehow cheated certain death. Why hadn't the lorry destroyed my car and me?

I sat at the wheel for what seemed an age, reeling from this second encounter with the unknown in twelve hours but, in this instance, I was centre stage rather than being an observer.

I looked in my driver's mirror and saw that my near smash had not gone unnoticed.

A police car slowly made its way towards me with its blue light flashing but no siren. It pulled up on the road behind me and a tall traffic policeman in a high visibility jacket got out and put a red triangle upright behind his car to alert drivers. Then he walked towards me. I wound down my window.

'You okay there, sir?' he asked, in a rising Scottish

burr.

'No, I didn't look properly, and this lorry went—'

'Where did you come from?' he asked, interrupting. 'I saw the lorry speeding down here but never saw your car. My car,' he pointed to a raised platform behind a clump of bushes, 'was in that speed trap just there. We get a lot of speeders on this road. 'Where are you going?'

'I'm trying to get to Perth and turned off for a rest but got confused by the junction. Then I looked right at the junction (lying) and then this lorry—.' I couldn't bring myself to tell him it had driven through my stationary car. How would that sound?

'Then you would have driven past me but I never saw you,' he broke in, getting out of his car and walking round to mine — what sounded like incredulity aimed as much at himself as me I thought.

He looked up and down the road, looking for inspiration probably. Muttering to himself, and probably noting his failings as an observant traffic cop, he made his way slowly round my car. Notes were jotted down in his notebook before he finally put one hand on my open window as I sat in my driver's seat. 'You go on your way,' he said, as his radio crackled with conversation from base. 'I want you to send me a written report of what *you* think happened when you get home, okay?' he said, giving me his card. 'This one's a bit of a weird one for me!'

I agreed and the policeman, before helping me reverse back onto the road, took a few photos of my car and the road in both directions. Stopping the traffic for a few moments was all I needed from him before I reversed back onto the main road to Aberdeen where I stayed with my brother's family for a few days.

My long drive back home to Buckinghamshire was uneventful and I pulled up outside my second floor flat as the sun was setting before the car park wall. I trudged upstairs with a couple of bags, opened the front door and saw I had a few letters waiting for me. Among the usual circulars there was a letter from the City of Perth Police. A bit unusual I thought in the age of email but a few minutes later I was in my living room with a cup of tea in hand perusing my post. I put down my tea before disbelief overtook me as I read the policeman's note.

'I took some pictures of your car for my report but what I found made no sense to me. There were no tyre tracks from your car pulling onto the verge. Makes no sense unless your car was dropped there from the sky, which is obviously impossible. What really got my attention was the photo I took of the interior; you were in the driver's seat but a tall figure dressed in white was sitting on your back seat. "He" seems to have something sprouting from his back but they can't be, and I am not saying any more. Have you seen him before? I have never seen anything like it, sir.'

I looked closely at the attached photo, mouth opening slowly.

It was the same figure I had seen in my bedroom.

20
The house of memories

Sixteen-year-old Jane went into her friend's bedroom on the first floor of a large Victorian villa to put a bit more make-up on so she could last out the party into the small hours.

It was dark outside, and the sounds of raucous party music drifted up the stairs from the smoky, spacious living room.

Jane couldn't wait to get back to the drinking and dancing as quickly as possible so, grabbing her lipstick, she began to rouge her lips, checking in the mirror she was doing it properly.

Momentarily glancing down at her hands to see if there was any red on them, she looked up at her reflection again.

A man in a blue military uniform was standing right behind her and smiling; his matching hat with gold braid throwing a shadow across the top of his face.

She tried to scream but froze.

She closed her eyes.

She opened her eyes.

He was still there, but now his face had become sad.

Somehow, she got up and, crashing into a double bed and side table, fled out of the room.

Because of the loud music no one had heard the commotion, but her pale face and shaking hands immediately alerted her friend Debbie, who was hosting the party.

Taking Jane aside, Debbie led her away from semi-drunken revellers who thronged around her, too befuddled by drink to be able to understand her fear or empathise; she, a fellow teen, albeit with a millionaire daddy, was now completely sober with a concerned face as she sat Jane down in the kitchen and made coffee.

Putting her coffee mug down soon after, she picked up Jane's hands and held them in front of her.

'You've seen him, haven't you?' Debbie said quietly.

Jane started to cry and shake anew.

'You know about him, right?'

'Yes,' Debbie poured out apologies, trying to make amends. 'We don't know who he is or even why he's here,' she continued. 'I didn't want to tell you or anyone in case I end up in a big house with no friends.'

'It's not a good secret to have Debbie,' Jane sniffed, her anger towards her friend dissipating as she relayed exactly what she had seen.

Telling the odd party goer who put their head round the door to go back to the party, the genial host soon after called a taxi to take Jane home and insisted on paying.

In the next few days as word of Jane's experience spread around school and their families, the identity of the nocturnal visitor became the cause of much speculation. Mostly, however, it was a mystery. Then, the following week, Jane was again invited to Debbie's house by Debbie's parents who were anxious to help try and solve the mystery so no one else would have the same experience.

'I've seen this man, mainly in the bedroom you went into,' Debbie's mum, Tina, said as they sat in the comfortable living room overlooking a well rolled lawn and a large, though overgrown, orchard in the background. 'He's always in the corner of my eye as a rule. Tony,' and here indicated her husband, 'has seen him a few times in the garden, but always from a distance. No one has seen him as close up as you. You must have attracted his attention,' she said, trying to attempt a joke but quickly realising no one was laughing.

Events subsequently died down for a few days then…

Jane started to have a recurring dream.

She was back in the bedroom at the house where she saw *him*.

Except it was a different period of time, though it was the recent past.

There was a young woman with her face hidden, sitting at a dressing table in the exact place Jane had been sitting all those years later.

The young woman was weeping over an open book, but Jane couldn't make out any writing.

As she came closer to the woman in her dream, the woman turned round, red eyed and showed her the book, then looked towards the bay window.

Then, invariably, Jane woke up.

After having this dream a couple of times, Jane was becoming depressed by it, but also concerned.

She had to tell Debbie.

Debbie was surprised by Jane's account. Who was the woman? Why was she crying? She obviously had some connection with the house at some point in the recent past before Debbie's parents had bought it in the 1960s.

The following week, emboldened by her new information, Jane forgot her fear of the ghost and returned with Debbie to Debbie's house in her dad's car after school. Debbie, her parents and Jane went upstairs into the large bedroom with the dressing table where she had seen the figure earlier, and Jane played out the events of her dream.

'The woman looks towards the window and downwards somehow,' Jane said, being drawn increasingly towards the frosted glass panes, starting to scrutinise their composition. 'The answer must be here,' she said, muttering to herself as she pottered around the bay window area.

They watched as Jane then started to kneel down at the skirting board, and felt impelled to pull up the faded green carpet. She then noticed one floorboard was loose.

'Look,' she said, as a six inch piece easily became free and she lifted it up.

Underneath, in the recess, caught by the daylight, was a faded, dusty book entitled in faded blue ink, 'Diary 1944.'

Jane leant down and picked it up, gently blowing off dust.

She opened the first page.

This diary belongs to Hannah Denton — secret!

It was the same book she had seen the young woman

looking at in the dream.

Debbie's parents came and stood next to Jane silently and somewhat reverently, not knowing what to make of this item that had lain under a floorboard undisturbed in their bedroom for so many years.

Jane then sat down and examined the pages; each covered with small, neat, blue script. Inevitably their curiosity focused on the last page and all three peered closer to read the entry:

'Dougie's plane lost over the channel. Am heartbroken.'

Small smudges of long lost tears could still be seen dotting the page accompanied by a small pencil drawing of two hearts with a cross inscribed through them.

'Oh my God,' Debbie's mother said quietly, taking the book in her hands and carefully looking through the pages, deciphering the faded ink script here and there. She then stopped, put the diary down and turned to her husband. 'We have to find out who Hannah is,' she said. 'And then we can find out who *he* is.'

'Know what?' said Jane looking up and anxiously around, glad she was in company. 'He's here now. I can tell.'

After a trip to the town library, Debbie's mother finally found and engaged a local researcher to try and unearth the truth about Hannah and, maybe, Dougie. Margaret Miller, a local lady, was no stranger to fishing about in dusky local and national archives and was apparently something of a medium in addition, a librarian had quietly informed Tina. Once Ms Miller had been engaged by Debbie's parents, the atmosphere at home had perceptibly lifted, in the knowledge that maybe these unfortunate souls could now be identified and helped in some way. Indeed, within the week Ms Miller had requested to meet the family at the house to see for herself the scene of Jane's encounter and offer some kind of *modus operandi*.

On a fine Saturday morning, Ms Miller appeared at the front door of Tony and Tina's house with a no nonsense demeanour and a determination to help the family and the house too; both needed it she concluded.

'Oh, he's here all right,' she said, on being asked if she felt anything after crossing the threshold into the entrance hall. 'He's on the main stairs watching us.'

Debbie and her parents felt nothing, and saw nothing to their relief, but were content to receive their visitor into the conservatory attached to the living room.

After all were seated in comfortable bamboo chairs, Ms Miller pulled out a sheaf of papers along with a few photocopied photographs and spread them on the glass table in front of them.

'Do you know the history of the house?' she asked Debbie's father.

'No,' he replied, matter-of-factly. 'We bought it after it had been empty for a while, I remember that,' he said. 'The garden and orchard had been neglected for many years. We managed to fix up the lawn but never got round to the orchard. I always found it a bit spooky, to be honest.'

'Well,' Ms Miller continued, 'I found documents in the town archives about this house's use during the war as a Women's Auxiliary Hostel. They were uniformed, too, and did a lot of clerical work for the war effort gathering and writing reports, mainly for air force squadrons based around here then. I found a list of the women billeted here too, and there she is,' she said, pointing at one girl in a faded black and white group photograph from the war years. 'Notice where it was taken?'

'Oh yes,' Debbie's mother noticed with a growing realisation. 'Out in the garden, actually roughly where we are sitting now!'

'Ah ha,' Ms Miller replied. 'No conservatory then either! Well, I went through the wartime editions of the local paper that I could find from 1944, but some were missing,' she said. 'Then there was this entry,' she said, lowering her voice and sighing.

The newspaper report laid out the bare details of a death in the orchard, near to the house. It seemed one young woman, in anguish at the loss of her unnamed airman boyfriend on a raid over Germany, had hanged herself in despair from an apple tree in the orchard. The coroner had decided it was suicide, and there it seemed the matter had rested.

Ms Miller turned her head towards the stairs and exclaimed, 'We are all sorry for what happened to poor Hannah and yourself. We wish only peace for your souls and eternal rest in the light.'

Turning to the group again she pulled out a small square sepia picture of a young woman in army uniform wearing a flat military cap. 'I found this photograph of Hannah. Notice anything again?'

'Oh my God, it's Jane,' Debbie said slowly, mouth

dropping.

Upstairs a door slammed.

'Oh, that poor girl — the resemblance is uncanny,' Tina said quietly, not immediately clear whether she was referring to Hannah or Jane. 'When Jane went into the bedroom at the party *he* must have thought it was his Hannah returned.'

'It's okay now,' Ms Miller said finally standing up to the assembled group. 'He's gone now. I sent him on his way to find Hannah and the light.'

Tina sighed again and reached for the drinks' cabinet. Her husband had beaten her to it, and poured himself a large whisky.

Debbie, however, didn't really know whether her family's troubles were really over, but did come to one decision. 'I do think that we should put the book back where Jane found it,' she said. 'It belongs to Hannah, not us.'

This was agreed on by all four and immediately carried out.

There the session ended with due gratitude on the part of the home owners and Ms Miller left, pleased at the outcome of her task. Jane was soon informed of recent events at the house and invited up again. On arrival in the hall, Jane immediately remarked to Debbie and her mum that the house seemed more peaceful and was pleased to stay for dinner.

Many years later Jane, grown up, had unfortunately lost touch with Debbie. She had chanced to drive past the scene where the events above had occurred long ago in the late 70s.

The house had been demolished, the neat garden

grubbed up.

The orchard, too, had gone. The whole area was now farmland and rough pasture. As the buildings had gone, so too the restless spirits hopefully, she thought driving away.